The
History
Mystery

Little Island received financial assistance from
The Arts Council (An Chomhairle Ealaíon), Dublin, Ireland.

 MINISTÉRIO DA CULTURA
Fundação BIBLIOTECA NACIONAL

The translation of this work was supported by a grant from the Ministério
da Cultura do Brasil / Fundação Biblioteca Nacional.
Obra publicada com o apoio do Ministério da Cultura do Brasil / Fundação

The History Mystery

Ana Maria Machado

Translated by Luisa Baeta

Little Island

THE HISTORY MYSTERY
Published 2012
by Little Island
7 Kenilworth Park
Dublin 6W
Ireland
www.littleisland.ie

First published as *Mensagem para você* by Editora Ática in São Paulo in 2008

Copyright © Ana Maria Machado 2007
Translation copyright © Luisa Baeta 2012

The author has asserted her moral rights.

ISBN 978-1-908195-22-7

Cover design and typeset by redrattledesign.com
Printed in Poland by Drukarnia Skleniarz

10 9 8 7 6 5 4 3

Contents

1. Project Mystery   1

2. Nefertiti   8

3. The Brainy Joker Strikes Again   14

4. A Clue – Maybe   24

5. Double Trouble   37

6. A Matter of Strategy   45

7. Message in a Bottle   62

8. Model What?   75

9. Camille's Friend   87

10. Rhythm, Poetry and Death   103

11. A Frozen Window   113

12. Gregorio Alvarenga's Dedication   124

13. Like a Movie   140

Think About It!   149

1. Project Mystery   151

2. Nefertiti   153

3. The Brainy Joker Strikes Again   155

4. A Clue – Maybe   157

5. Double Trouble   158

6. A Matter of Strategy   159

7. Message in a Bottle   161

8. Model What?   162

9. Camille's Friend   163

10. Rhythm, Poetry and Death   165

11. A Frozen Window   166

12. Gregorio Alvarenga's Dedication   167

13. Like a Movie   168

Answers to Think About It
3 – The Brainy Joker Strikes Again   169

Answers to quiz   170

About the Author

Ana Maria Machado was born in 1941 in Rio de Janeiro and is one of the most significant children's book authors in Brazil. She has written more than a hundred books for children and adults. She started her career as a painter, worked as a journalist for *Elle* magazine in Paris and for the BBC in London. In 1979, she opened the first children's literature bookshop in Brazil.

In the year 2000, Ana Maria Machado was awarded the Hans Christian Andersen Award, the most significant international prize for children's literature, for her life's work.

Before you start ...

This book was originally written in Brazilian Portuguese and published in Brazil. You might never have been there, though you might have seen TV programmes from or about Brazil, and you will know that it is a very large country in South America, and the only one where Portuguese is the main language. (You probably know what the main language is in the other countries of South America, so we don't need to tell you that.)

Brazil is an unusual country. It is vast, and there are parts of the country that are so far from the coast, it takes hours to get there, even by plane. It's also a very varied country. There are some extremely rich people in Brazil, and then also a lot of people living in poverty. It is a very racially mixed country as well, with people from all kinds of backgrounds. A lot of people live in the cities, of course, but there are also people living a traditional way of life in the remotest parts of the country, in the rainforest for example.

This book is set in the city, and life there is not all that different from life in the United States or Europe. Kids go to school and use computers and listen to music and visit each other's houses and so on. But as you read this book, it might be interesting to watch out for things you think are a bit different from the way you live.

So now you know a bit about Brazil – but actually, the first chapter is mostly about ancient Egypt!

Quiz on Brazil

(The answers are at the back of the book.)

1: What is the capital city of Brazil? (Watch out! It might not be the one you expect.)

2: What is the name of the famous city on the south coast with beautiful beaches and a famous statue of Christ the King? (Hint: there are three words in the name of this city.)

3: What is the main language of Brazil?

4: Brazil has always been very good at football. Has it ever won the World Cup?

5: Brazilians love to dance. What is the most famous kind of dancing from Brazil?

6: Brazil is famous for certain food products. Can you name one thing that comes from Brazil that you would find in most people's homes where you live?

1 – Project Mystery

'William's team has done the best project,' announced the history teacher.

Will could hardly believe his ears. The others must have been really terrible. He knew perfectly well that his team had made a mess of their time management, which meant they'd had to do a lot of the work in a rush at the end. The project had to have been pretty slapdash.

On the last day, they had been practically kicked out of Sonia's place by her mother because it was so late, and they still hadn't got as far as putting all the bits and pieces of work into the right order on the computer before printing it out. There was still a whole lot of stuff that needed to be finished. It just couldn't have turned out good. So how on earth could a teacher as demanding as Mr Costa possibly think their work was the best in the class?

Will stole a glance at Pedro, who had an even more amazed look on his face. And that same astonished expression was repeated on the faces of all the other members of the project team – Matt, Faye and Sonia.

Sonia's expression was the most amazed of all. She had her hand clapped across her open mouth and her eyes were wide with surprise. More than any of them, she knew that their project on the ancient Egyptians had been a patchwork of bits and pieces, all cobbled together any old way.

Mr Costa continued with his feedback: 'Although it is poorly structured ...'

For sure, they all thought. It really was a total mess. '... the work was very interesting and quite original ...'

Who ever would have thought it!

'... especially the part about Akhenaten's monotheistic experience.'

Wait ... What? Who did that bit? I never even saw it! was the thought going through all the teammates' minds.

Sonia remembered how she had stayed up until almost four in the morning working on the computer after her classmates had left. She was so tired, she could barely concentrate enough to put the pages in order. And in the end there had been an extra bit of material that she had been unable to identify. Sonia didn't know which of her teammates had written that part and sent it to her, how it had appeared there or even what it was about. She couldn't find a way to make it fit in with the rest of the work and ended up leaving it out, like in one of those cartoons where somebody tries to fix a clock and when they've finished they realise there are a couple of nuts and bolts left over.

'The only reason you are not getting an A+ for this is that it is sometimes slightly confused ...'

Slightly? It's totally confused, they all thought.

'... and because it doesn't refer to the sources used in this part of the research. But the idea of including this theme in your project was really creative, and the subject was very well introduced. I will read the beginning out loud so the whole class can see what I mean.'

None of the team had any idea what Mr Costa was talking about, but the teacher cleared his throat and began reading.

'"Although in your day ..."' he began. 'Meaning *our* day,' he muttered. 'I missed this error the first time I read it ...'

He stopped and made a correction on the page with a pen, then carried on.

'"Although in our day the name of the pharaoh Tutankhamun has become very well known and he has become a real celebrity, due to the discovery of his tomb and the fantastic fortune of the treasure enclosed with it, the truth is that for the people of his time he was not very important.

'"He started to rule while he was still a teenager, and he was weak, sickly and passive. He reigned only for a short period of time and died before turning twenty. He came to the throne through a series of court intrigues, and was simply a puppet in the hands of political and religious forces interested in reclaiming the power that Akhenaten, the deposed pharaoh, had ..."'

The friends exchanged glances. They'd never even heard of this Akhen-whatever-his-name-was.

"'But history has not forgotten Akhenaten,'" Mr Costa was droning on. "'He was a cultured man, a thinker. With him, for the first time, the idea of a single god was formulated – Aten, the Sun-god, the source of light, heat and life. Akhenaten showed a mind way ahead of his time.'"

While Mr Costa went on reading, the people on William's team continued to look at each other in amazement. None of them had researched that. *It must have been Sonia*, the others thought. After they'd left, she must have found that part in some book or online and stuck it in without telling them. Luckily, it had worked like a charm.

"'He also valued the role of women: his wife, Queen Nefertiti, had an active part in government. She was able to read and composed many religious hymns and poems celebrating Aten.'"

'I'm not going to read the whole paper now,' Mr Costa said. 'I just wanted to give you all a little taste of it. I even learned a few things myself from this project. I have to admit that I didn't know much about Nefertiti, except that she was married to Akhenaten and that she was very beautiful.'

Somebody must have made a smart remark, because laughter could be heard from the back of the class. But Mr Costa took no notice and carried on, all excited.

'Yes. A model of Nefertiti's head, in a museum in Berlin, is one of the most gorgeous and well-preserved objects we have from the ancient world. But I had no idea about the intellectual role Nefertiti played. I looked all this stuff up and found that what you say here is quite accurate. But tell me, where did you find all of this information?'

Silence.

The teacher repeated the question and William answered vaguely, 'Well, Mr Costa ... we researched so much stuff it's hard to remember. Maybe one of us wrote down the source somewhere, but I think possibly it got thrown out by accident. Sorry about that.'

'That's a shame, William,' said Mr Costa. 'These things should not happen. As I always say, it's OK to do your research on the internet, but you always have to quote your sources so that I can check if they are reliable.'

There he goes again, thought William. Mr Costa was always banging on about how the most important thing that the school can teach is not the facts, but the 'formation of dignified social attitudes' and the 'transmission of ethical values' and 'rigour and enthusiasm in the search for knowledge', blah, blah, blah.

They'd all heard that speech a thousand times. Once he got started on it, it seemed like he was never going to let up.

'That's why a bibliography is essential too,' Mr Costa was saying. 'You always need to identify the source and quote the reference.'

William disconnected mentally and started thinking how he was going to get to the next level in a new computer game he'd got two days before. Faye was sketching on a piece of paper as usual, playing at being a fashion designer. And Matt was dreaming about the sandwich he was going to have at break, because he was starving.

When break-time finally came, everyone gathered around Sonia.

'Hey, thanks, you saved the day!'

'Where did you get that sun-god stuff?' asked Matt.

'And the thing about the model of beauty?' Faye was probably going to ask about make-up or fashion in ancient Egypt. That's all she ever thought about.

'I have no idea,' Sonia answered.

At first they didn't believe her, but Sonia insisted it was true.

'After I had printed everything out, I went to bed, and next morning, I was in a rush to gather up the pages before school, and I noticed some weird stuff that I didn't remember seeing before or talking to any of you about. I thought it must be something one of you had sent on by email. I took out one bit that looked completely random, but I left the bit about that pharaoh in, because it was about ancient Egypt, and that was what we were supposed to be writing about. Our project was way too short, so I thought maybe something about some pharaoh would be useful to pad it out.'

'What about the other bit, the stuff you took out?' asked Matt. 'Any chance you might have downloaded a ready-made chemistry project too? We have to hand in Ms Nancy's work at the end of the month.'

'No such luck,' said Sonia with a grin. 'There was nothing like that. There were some poems, a letter — I'm not sure what, exactly. It was nonsense. I threw it all away.'

2 – Nefertiti

When she got home, Sonia was still wondering about those other pages. She was curious now and wanted to read the material again. She shouldn't have thrown it all out without a second thought.

But had she actually thrown the pages out? Maybe she'd just left them on the scrap-paper pile beside the printer. Everyone in their house did that with paper that was only printed on one side.

Sure enough, she found the missing pages in the pile of scrap paper. She couldn't be sure it was all there, but she recognised one of the poems because it was printed in the same font that she'd used for the project for Mr Costa.

> Every day as you arrive
> And call us with birds' songs,
> All in you is joy,
> Oh one god who dries our tears!
> Oh god who hears the silence of the poor!
> Oh beautiful and magnificent!
> Each day as you unwrap your cloth of light

And warm the world with the heat of your rays,
All in you brings life,
Oh one god who feeds us!
Oh god who ripens the harvest!
Oh beautiful and magnificent!

There were lots more verses like that. There was also a letter. Or … not exactly a letter – there was no date, address or signature. It wasn't an email either – there was none of the usual stuff you get at the top of an email. But it seemed like a letter because it was written in the first person and was clearly addressed to someone.

I'm sorry, I know I should not stick my nose into this, but you are so tired that I wanted to help you. Forgive me.

This sounded as if the person was talking directly to Sonia herself!

I remembered my own daughters, so dear, whom I loved to play with and to whom I always enjoyed teaching everything. Since I have decided to speak out, though, I will tell the truth. It is more than just a desire to help. It is also a desire to show off a little. And I want to show off because I am very proud of knowing how to write, as you can imagine.

Well, Sonia couldn't really imagine, but she read on.

I am always thankful to my father for having the courage to teach me. First, one would be taught how to draw. Always the first step, and an essential one. I had a beautiful little case, made of wood, thin and long, where I could keep the quills – that you would later call brushes or pens, I believe. They were made of reed. Some had their tips flattened, opening like a fan, and were good for painting. The tips of the other ones were made into a point, becoming thin and better for drawing lines. The lid of my little case would slide out, opening to reveal four rounded hollows where I kept the pigments.

My father's case had nine hollows because, as he worked for the palace, he used many colours. Most scribes had only two: black and red. This case was one of my greatest treasures, even considering all the amazing wonders I had after growing up.

I have always loved drawing and painting, and I would use any shell, any piece of rock or clay, to practise. My mother allowed me to paint some of the walls in our house. Her favourite picture was of a hippopotamus in the water, with his mouth open. The one I liked the most was of a bird among the reeds, by the river. It was very important to be able to paint and draw well if you wanted to learn how to write in a way that everybody could understand.

That's because our writing was made of drawings, and not of letters like yours.

And not all the symbols were as simple as the sun disc. Can you imagine if someone wanted to draw a jackal and a cat came out? Or drew a falcon that looked like a quail? It would change the meaning completely and become a different word. That is why I had to practise so much.

When I was almost the size of your younger sister …

Sonia *did* have a younger sister. Was this woman really speaking to *her*?

… my father taught me to sit on the floor with my legs crossed, as scribes are supposed to do, to unroll the papyrus and start drawing the symbols carefully, from the top down, from right to left. Slowly, I learned to form the words. My father was a palace scribe, an important man, and he taught me well how to hold the reed correctly and perform the gestures with precision.

The scribes were always men. I knew that my father's decision was an act of courage and love: teaching a girl to read and write. That was why, after I grew up and got married, I could do something very good: writing the words of the hymns I made up and sang myself. Playing, singing and dancing was part of girls' education. It was like sewing and embroidering. But reading and writing? Very few could do it. I thank my father.

I have never felt so important as on the day when I could write my own name and, when it was done, trace firmly the cartouche, the rounded frame we use around people's names, to protect it. You cannot do it now on your computer. But if you would like to see, I will leave you a link here. Just visit the website and browse until you find my name, 'Nefertiti'.

Someone is playing a weird joke on me, thought Sonia. She decided it was best not to mention this to anyone, but instead wait to see if the joker would show up again.

But there was nothing to stop her from following the link, which was to the website for some museum, the Egyptology section. More specifically, it was about Egyptian writing.

The webpage had a whole lot of stuff about hieroglyphics, the symbols used for writing in ancient Egypt. There was a list with lots of little drawings and their corresponding sounds in modern languages. And there were some more general explanations, such as the information about how names of people were circled with an oval-shaped frame, or rather a rectangular frame with rounded edges, with a straight line on the base. The so-called cartouche. Just as the message that Sonia had got had described.

Then she saw something that made her curious. On a corner of the page, there was a sentence that read: *Do you want to see how some famous names were spelled? Click here!*

She clicked and up came a list: Cleopatra, Ptolemy, Rameses, Tutankhamun, Tutmes … and there in the middle, as if it were winking at her, Nefertiti. Sonia selected and clicked again. The screen showed:

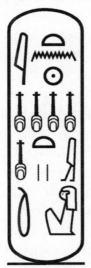

This must be some brainy joker! Sonia was definitely not going to make a fool of herself by telling the others about this, but she was curious now to know who was trying to have fun at her expense.

3 – The Brainy Joker Strikes Again

'Bye, I'm running late!'

Sonia's older sister, Andrea, was rushing to catch her lift to work. 'Colin will be here any minute now.'

It was the same thing every morning. The alarm clock would ring but Andrea didn't get up right away. She stayed in bed for ages, snoozing and stretching. Then, all of a sudden, it was like someone had plugged Andrea in. She would sprint into the bathroom, turn on some upbeat music, take a shower, get dressed in minutes and would be running from one place to another without even having time to sit down and have her breakfast properly. She would swallow half a glass of milk and rush out with a biscuit or a piece of fruit in her hand to get her lift with Colin to Dr Barry's law firm. You'd think it was the most desirable job in the world, in the most important company on the planet, but actually she was just an intern.

This morning, though, Andrea took a moment to catch her breath before running out the door. She turned to her two sisters, who were sitting at the table, and said, 'By the way, Sonia, I've been meaning to tell you for days and keep forgetting, I think your computer has a virus.'

Sonia was running late too but, unlike her sister, she was still half-asleep at the table. She couldn't understand how Andrea could be this electric when she woke up, talking her head off. Sonia was much slower: she woke up gradually, slow and steady.

But this piece of information woke her up all right. *A virus? Oh, no! Let's hope it isn't true, or at least let it be nothing too serious.* Her computer had never been infected by a virus, but she'd heard some awful stories. She would have to call Pedro so he could reformat the hard drive, like he'd done with Matt's computer when he'd had problems. Pedro was great with technology. Come to think of it, calling Pedro for help was really an excellent idea, even if there turned out to be no virus. It was a good excuse to get him to come to her house.

She took a little sip of her tea. *Ah, good.* It was finally at the temperature she liked: not so hot that it burned your tongue, not so cold that it tasted bad. Just right.

She sighed and thought about Pedro again. Or still.

This had been happening a lot lately. She kept catching herself thinking about Pedro. Like the tea, he too was just right. But what should you do when you find out that your best friend, your classmate for years, is suddenly more to you than just a friend?

A new boy would be easier – there's an exchange of looks, some flirting. It becomes clear to both people. It's part of what everybody expects: two people meet, like each other, things can happen. But what about somebody who's been in your class your whole life, since your first day at school? It's hard to change all of a sudden.

Maybe she would need that thing they had been talking about the other day in literature class: a new image, seeing the familiar in a fresh way, the kind of thing advertisers are good at.

'... but on ours?' Carol's voice interrupted Sonia's thoughts.

'What did you say?' Sonia asked her little sister.

'You were really in another world, weren't you? It's like you don't care about what your sisters have to say.'

'Don't start, Carol. What do my sisters have to do with anything?'

'Everything! Your older sister just said our computer has a virus. And your younger sister has been asking how she even knows that? Andrea shouldn't be messing around with our stuff. She's got her own computer.'

That was true. The family had a better, newer, faster computer that, in theory, they all shared in their dad's study. But Andrea had taken it over. All that was left for the two younger sisters was the old PC, which had been put in their room. It really was a dinosaur and took hours downloading anything. But there was an advantage: it belonged to the two of them and them alone. Andrea didn't need to use it. Apart from the family computer, she also had a computer at the company where she was doing work experience. And her boyfriend was always offering to let her use his laptop. So why on earth had she been sticking her nose into their computer?

'Fair enough,' said Sonia. 'You're right. I'll have to ask Andrea about that.'

'Not just *ask*,' Carol corrected her. 'You need to give her a good telling off.'

'OK, leave it to me. I'll have a serious talk with Andrea. I'll do it today.'

It wasn't until the next day that Sonia got a chance to speak to Andrea, however, because Andrea was late home that evening. So they didn't meet again until the following morning, once again over breakfast at the kitchen table. Sonia would have forgotten all about it, she was so sleepy in the mornings, but Carol wouldn't let it go.

'Andrea, Sonia wants to talk to you about our computer.'

That seemed to set Andrea off. She started gabbling.

'I'm glad you brought this up. I've been wanting to have this out with you two. Computers are not kids' toys, you know, and they're expensive. If you have a problem, you should call technical support right away.'

The conversation was not going the way Carol had planned. The two younger girls could hardly get a word in edgeways, and it was all the wrong way around. The one who was doing the telling off was Andrea. That wasn't how it was supposed to go.

'At first I thought it was just nonsense,' Andrea was babbling on, 'a stupid virus, because of those weird little symbols that appeared on the screen. That's why I said that thing yesterday morning. Only later, when I got to the office and started revising the terms of a petition with Colin, he noticed something strange and asked me what that was doing in the middle of my work. I was *so* embarrassed! There I was, concentrating on serious stuff, work stuff, and looking like a fool … I had this really well-grounded argument, based on a long history of jurisprudence and case histories, and then in the middle of it comes all this rubbish from you girls. Colin was really sweet about it, but of course he thought it was weird. Frankly, girls …'

'Can you explain exactly what happened?' Sonia was trying to sound focused.

Putting her empty glass on the table and getting ready to leave, Andrea said, 'I spent *days* researching this stuff. I went to a lot of trouble. I even found precedents for our argument in ancient Roman law, in Hammurabi's code …'

Whose code? Sonia had never heard of the guy.

'... in lots of places, and then there was all that childish nonsense scattered in the middle of it. It was lucky that Colin noticed it before we handed it all to Dr Barry, otherwise ...'

While she was talking, Andrea was fussing with her folder. She shuffled a few sheets of paper, then took two pages and left them on the kitchen counter, putting the sugar bowl on top of them so they wouldn't fly away. Before either of her younger sisters had time to say anything, she had already picked an apple out of the basket on the table and was standing on the threshold, about to sink her teeth into the fruit and disappear from sight on her way to work.

She snapped, 'I should have thrown it away, of course. I just kept it out of the goodness of my heart. There it is. I'm in a hurry. Bye!'

And she was gone.

'You didn't even ask what she was doing on our computer!' Carol complained. 'She can't just –'

'Shut up, Carol,' Sonia interrupted, getting up slowly and walking to the counter.

Carol was used to Sonia's foul mood in the mornings so she didn't say anything, but she was surprised to see her sister getting up and picking up the sheets of paper. Kind of looking like a zombie, it's true. Still, she was moving a lot more than usual for that time of the morning.

Sonia sat down with the pages in her hand and examined them carefully. On the first page was a list. A shopping list, perhaps, but quite weird. There were some insane items, some crazy amounts and some nonsense prices in a very strange currency. But it couldn't be a shopping list. Nobody writes down the price of something in order to remember to buy it. So what could this list be for?

30 sheep
20 packs of Anatolian wool
2 combs for wool
2 hair combs
3 wooden spoons
2 wooden looms
1 wooden container full of spindles
15 good quality cloths

Carol was on tenterhooks, but Sonia read in silence. She didn't say a word, intrigued with the whole thing. Combs for wool and hair combs? What on earth was that? Perhaps somebody wanted to comb a sheep? Or comb the yarn made on one of those wooden looms?

She moved on to the next page. There was a message like that Egyptian one that had appeared in the history project: no sign of being an email and no letterhead this time either. This time, it started with the kind of language Andrea used at her work. But it soon changed:

Once again I apologise for the intrusion and insistence. However, I hope that with the repetition of this procedure I may count on your understanding.

It gives me great satisfaction to verify that our juridic model continues to interest you, even after such a length of time. We are all very proud of the codification work that the great king Hammurabi, shepherd of our salvation, has done by gathering in writing the laws that bind us, so as to orient the strict discipline and good conduct of our people.

But I would like to tell you something of which I am deeply proud: I am a woman and a commoner, but I too can write. This is my personal pride. I do not know how to use the complicated terms of the codes (or did not know, but now, in these ethereal waves, any scribe absorbs every language around, in a virtual state, so I can attempt it). I have never had the scribe profession, mother of eloquence, father of knowledge, a delight from which one never gets tired, to quote a poem written to its glory. I have learned, however, the basic concepts and could always form in the clay tablets the essential words of my role.

When my husband left in a caravan to do business with merchants from other lands, I was the one in charge of writing the messages necessary for his commercial contracts, and also the one who kept in order all the accounting from our business, especially that which referred to the textiles. I was the one who reminded him of exactly which merchandise another merchant was taking in the caravan and still owed us money for, for example.

That must be what the list was about, Sonia thought. Something to do with keeping track of the goods for sale.

And I was not the only one. A few other women also did this – after all, we were the ones who have always woven and understood textiles and yarns. It was our production. It has always been so. This is why, among our people – who invented writing before anyone else, it's worth remembering – several feminine hands learned to use the different kinds of reed we needed. Sharp for scratching, with a triangular tip to engrave the characters in the soft clay, or with a round tip for the numbers.

But none of this matters now. My knowledge grows and transforms into any writing that may reach you by computer. Today I wished to show you that I can write and how happy this makes me. A happiness that remains throughout the centuries, even though I myself do not write codes and

understand that it is merely research that brings
you close to me now, from a time in which women
can study codes, write laws or judge.

That was it. There was nothing more. Maybe there
had been another page, which Andrea had not kept.
Maybe not.

Once again, what Sonia had in front of her was
not exactly a letter or an email, but a message from
someone who addressed the reader directly. But
this communication didn't seem to be from Nefertiti
or have anything to do with Egypt. Instead, it was
full of all that stuff about lawyers and codes and
said something about this Hammurabi person that
Andrea had also mentioned. Why?

The Brainy Joker had clearly struck again. But
there were new clues here. Sonia was more curious
than ever now. She would definitely talk to Pedro
about this and ask for his help.

4 – A Clue – Maybe

'You know something? This sounds like a virus – and possibly one I've come across before.'

Sonia was doubly happy when she heard Pedro say that. She had just told him she'd been getting these weird messages through her computer that seemed to be coming from someone claiming to be from another era. She had been half afraid her friend would laugh at her and not take it seriously. So it was a relief to hear that someone else had come up against something like this before. And it was really good that Pedro had some experience of a virus like this. That might help.

Before she even had time to invite him to her house to see the computer, he was already offering.

'Can I come over and take a look?'

'Of course you can. Any time you like!'

'I'm really curious,' Pedro said. 'Maybe I can get a better grasp of it this time. Last time, I didn't get anywhere with it.'

'Oh, what happened?'

'Luckily, the problem disappeared out of the blue,

just as randomly as it had appeared. I didn't even get a chance to show it to the school's IT support guys.'

'But why would you want to show it to the school?' asked Sonia, mystified.

'Because it was on one of the PCs in the computer lab at school that I came across it. Didn't I say that already?'

No, he had not. And there were other things that Pedro had not explained either, that came out bit by bit as they talked.

He explained that the problem had happened at Garibaldi High School, on one of the shared computers in the lab. Those PCs never rested. Dozens of kids took turns on them for schoolwork.

'But what exactly happened?' she asked.

He countered with another question: 'Do you know Robbie?'

'Of course, Pedro, who doesn't know Robbie?'

Robbie was not a student at their school, but everyone there knew him. One of the things about Garibaldi High that the school was especially proud of were the after-hours community classes taught by the students themselves to underprivileged kids. The school made the classrooms available and students volunteered to teach classes in the subjects they were good at (such as the piano or French or maths – Sonia taught history on Wednesdays), while the school's regular teachers gave them support.

The idea was for the students to do voluntary work in an extracurricular activity that would look good on their CVs later on, while helping out young people who lived in a neighbourhood where the schools were not so well funded by the government. Robbie worked part-time in the school cafeteria and was one of Sonia's students in her Wednesday history class – a good student, it had to be said. In addition to that, he was an excellent football player and was often seen playing with the students in the Garibaldi High gymnasium. Every now and then, when they played a match against another school, the PE teachers would sneak Robbie in to play for the school's team. Then they would all head out together to celebrate the victory or forget the defeat. So Robbie was practically a celebrity in the school, although he wasn't technically a Garibaldi student.

'Well, the problem with the school computer actually happened with Robbie,' Pedro was saying. 'He had a new song and wanted to print a few copies of the lyrics for the rest of the band.'

That made sense, because not only was he a good football player, Robbie was also a songwriter and he hosted a council-supported internet radio show – he had been writing some wicked rap songs lately.

'So he asked me to take the lyrics home with me,' Pedro continued, 'type them up and print out a few copies for him. But I thought we could just use the computer lab in the school. That would be quicker and more practical, so I asked Joe and he said that was OK.

'Robbie is not exactly a computer whizz, though. He doesn't own a computer and he gets some of the commands muddled up sometimes, so I thought it would be good to stay with him while he was doing it.'

Sonia nodded. She wished he would get to the point, but at the same time, she liked listening to his voice.

'So, we had been in the lab for about half an hour, the two of us on different computers, when he called me over, saying something weird was happening.

'He had typed in the lyrics, all with short lines – you know, poetry-style – but when he was sending it to print, he must have hit the wrong key and something else appeared, a load of long lines that filled the screen right out to the edge.

'I thought it was just a layout problem, so I sat down next to him to take a look. But it really was a completely different piece of writing. In fact, *two* different things appeared.'

'Oh?'

'Yes. First, there was a story about an old man who lived high up in the mountains and had a couple of assassins working for him, to help keep control of his "merchandise" ...'

'Oh, Pedro, that's rough,' said Sonia. She had

jumped to the conclusion that the word 'merchandise' referred to the drug-dealing that everyone knew went on around the area where Robbie lived.

'Yeah, well, that's what I thought too when I read it. It was kind of scary, actually. I thought some of these gangsters had somehow broken into the school network.'

Sonia shook her head.

'I actually thought it was some kind of threat,' Pedro was saying. 'I thought it was a response to Robbie's lyrics about living in peace, without violence: "Ya wanna live in peace and ya say ya don't know how, Well bro, let me tell ya, I'm gonna tell ya now". That's how it starts. But maybe these guys didn't like that idea, wanted to warn him off or something? I don't know.'

'But that wasn't it?'

'I really don't know, Sonia. This thing that came up on the screen used some weird words. I mean, it talked about delivering the merchandise by *caravan*. Bits of it did seem to be about drug-dealing and gang stuff, but then other parts seemed to be from another planet.'

'How do you mean?'

'Hold on, I'm getting there. So when that page was finished, I scrolled down, and the next bit was a letter.'

'Like, an email?'

'No. A letter or a message, only it didn't say who it

was for, and it didn't have a signature. But the person explained that, when he was a boy, about our age, he went travelling around the world with his dad and his uncle. He lived for many years in distant countries, he said, and he had crossed deserts and mountains, seas and forests, and reached a different ocean.'

'Hmm,' said Sonia. 'I see what you mean about being from a different planet. Doesn't have anything to do with life around Robbie's area, anyway.'

'He "saw many wonders", he said, and he had been an ambassador for a great oriental king. He was bragging about lots of stuff. I can't even remember it all any more.'

'Weird,' said Sonia.

'Yeah, and according to himself, he invented pasta, or something like that.'

'Pasta?'

'And another thing I remember, because he kept repeating it every five lines or so: he was very proud of knowing how to write and he kept boasting about it and trying to show off about it to us. He said he'd written this great book that was a big success, all about his travels.'

'That's a bit like my Brainy Joker,' added Sonia.

'Exactly. That struck me too, when you told me about those messages you got. That's what made me remember.'

Sonia was puzzled.

'Anyway, listen,' Pedro went on, 'it's coming back to me. This guy also said that many years later, when he was old and came back from his travels, he was arrested. He said that he wrote this book of his while he was in prison. He didn't actually write it down himself though. He dictated it to a cell companion who was a professional scribe.'

'Hey,' said Sonia, 'I wish I had read that message. You didn't print it out, did you?'

'It never even crossed my mind,' said Pedro. 'At that moment, I just wanted to get rid of the message and get back to the page with Robbie's lyrics. I did read the pages, but then I closed them. I didn't think to save the message, so it must have disappeared.'

Sonia was disappointed. She had been getting excited about the idea of comparing her own two messages with this new one.

'What about the IT support guys?' she suggested.

'Well, I didn't go into too much detail with them. I was afraid of getting Robbie into trouble. If they thought he'd brought a virus in, they probably wouldn't let him use the school computers any more or something. So I just kind of mentioned it to Joe – I was pretty vague about it, and he told me not to worry, he'd take a look.'

'And he didn't find anything?' Sonia asked, more hopeful now. Joe was an absolute expert on computers: that was his job. He would definitely find anything that was to be found.

'Well,' said Pedro, 'the next day he just said that he hadn't found anything wrong. He thought it was probably just some other student's project, someone who'd used the computer before us and whose essay we ended up erasing. Whoever it was, they were probably going to be furious about it. So we waited for another student to complain.'

Pedro talked so slowly. Sonia was impatient. She tried to speed him up.

'And then?'

'And then nothing. That was it. Until today, when you told me the secret about our wonderful team project about ancient Egypt. And this story about your sister and the letter from the woman who wrote shopping lists.'

Sonia looked at him. She wasn't convinced that that was all he had to say.

'Come on, Pedro, I trusted you. I told you something that I have not told anyone else. But I know you — we've been friends for ever — and I could bet money that you're holding something back.'

Pedro stared at the ground for a little while. Then he looked into Sonia's eyes, gave one of those smiles that could melt ice, and confessed.

'Yeah, you're right, I do have an idea, but I'm not sure about it. It's not that I don't trust you, Sonia, because I do. You're my friend and you're a really special girl. But the thing is, I may be wrong and

I might end up being unfair to someone, and that's why I didn't want to say anything more.'

Wrong? How? thought Sonia. *You just said I'm a really special girl, and there's nothing wrong with that. Things have never felt so right in all my life.*

'See, in my opinion, it's not a virus, Sonia. I think we're dealing with a hacker. You know what that is, right? Those guys who can break into other people's computer networks.'

'Of course I know that. I've heard of hacking.'

'But the thing is, hacking is illegal. That's why I didn't want to say anything about it until I was pretty sure.'

'I see, yeah. It's not nice, is it? Though it's probably just a joke, don't you think?'

'It's a *crime*, Sonia. I mean, suppose this person is part of one of these criminal organisations that steal money from banks or sabotage companies and stuff like that?'

'You mean, it could be *dangerous*?'

'Well, in theory, yeah, it could be. But in this case, I don't really think so. I think you're right that this person is really just messing around, playing some stupid joke. Still, I can't resist wanting to find out more, can you? And now that we have a few different messages to go on, I think we're starting to piece a few things together about this Brainy Joker of yours.'

Sonia was just about to say something when Pedro

gave a start. 'Oh! I've just remembered something else. In that message Robbie and I got, the guy said he was from Venice.'

'Do you think it's an Italian, then? Could that be why his use of language is strange? He could be lying about that, though, to cover up ...'

There were so many ideas tumbling around in Sonia's head all at once, she could hardly get them all out.

'Hey, listen, Sonia. I've just worked something out! Think about it. We know who this fellow from Venice is, because we happen to have learned about him and his voyages.'

'Do we? Did we? Who?'

'Remember?' said Pedro. 'In one of the books that we read in history last year ...'

Sonia thought about it but nothing came to mind, though it did ring a vague bell. Pedro kept trying to ring that bell a little louder.

'Come on, Sonia. Who was the great traveller who left Venice as a kid, journeyed all through the East, was an ambassador for the emperor Kublai Khan and on his way home was arrested and, in prison, wrote the *Book of the Marvels of the World*?'

'Marco Polo!' she cried. 'How come I didn't think of that before?'

'But listen, *we* know that, right, because we did it at school. But a lot of people wouldn't know it.'

'So that makes us smart, is that it?'

'No, that's not the point. The thing is, it wouldn't make any sense to use this story to play a joke on people who don't know anything about Marco Polo or who haven't been thinking about him quite recently. It only works on people in our actual class – people who have the right information to understand what the message is about.'

'OK, but I still don't understand how this might be a clue.'

Pedro hesitated before continuing.

'Well ... it's a only a little clue. It may be nothing, really. But this joker or hacker or whatever already mentioned Egypt and Nefertiti just as we were working on ancient Egypt. Then he went for the Hammurabi code with your sister, who's training to be a lawyer and knows all about laws and things, and then he starts talking about Marco Polo to me and Robbie. Do you remember how Marco Polo tells this story about an old man in the mountains who has all these killers at his service?'

Sonia nodded. It was coming back to her.

'Right, so when Robbie was writing his rap song that mentions assassins and merchandise, this person starts going on about assassins and merchandise too.'

'So?'

'Well, whenever he strikes, this joker, he's talking

about something that is related to *us*, somehow.'
Pedro paused, took a breath and went on. 'That's
why I'm thinking this must be someone who knows
us, Sonia. But also someone who has read quite a
few books and knows their history.'

'Hmm. A historian?'

'I'm starting to suspect Mr Costa, actually.'

'*Pedro!* Anyway, he doesn't know my sister. How
could he send her a message?'

'But if she was using your computer? He could have
hacked into it and he could have read the document
she was writing. And he could have seen that your
sister was doing research about Hammurabi, so
then he writes about that.'

'But then it could be anyone who can hack into
a computer,' Sonia argued. 'It doesn't have to be
someone who knows us, as long as they can pick up
on what we are working on.'

'No,' said Pedro. 'It's not that simple. Nobody
mentioned Marco Polo, but the Brainy Joker –
Brainy Hacker, whatever you want to call him or
her – used that story, knowing we'd know what he
was on about. That's why I suspect Mr Costa.'

'I really don't know, Pedro.' Sonia was not convinced.
'Why would Mr Costa do a thing like that? What's in
it for him? What's his interest in helping us out and
giving us such a good grade? Our team above all –
the one that probably did the worst project of the lot.'

It was Pedro's turn to think. 'Yeah ... you've got a point. It makes no sense. I hadn't thought about that. And anyway, it's not like Mr Costa. He loves the moral high ground. But this hacker *is* someone who knows his history very well. As well as Mr Costa does.'

They were silent for a while. Then Sonia made a suggestion.

'Let's go to my place so you can read the messages and take a good look at the computer. After that, I promise, I'm done exploiting you. We'll listen to this new album I just downloaded and we'll have something special to eat.'

Pedro seemed to get what she meant, because he smiled and said, 'Special? Like the two of us. Let's go!'

5 – Double Trouble

They read and reread the messages that had been left on the computer in Sonia's house. But try as they might, they couldn't reach a conclusion. So they decided to skip ahead to the special snack and the new music, along with very special talks as old friends with so much in common, who slowly start noticing new charms in each other.

Very slowly – way too slowly for Sonia's taste. By now she had no doubt that she was in fact starting to like Pedro very much and she really hoped he felt the same way about her. They ended up not talking any more about the mysterious Brainy Hacker. At least, not that afternoon.

For a few days, nothing new or strange happened with the computer and they gradually began to forget about the joker or hacker or whatever it was. It wasn't until Saturday of the following week that the subject came up again – twice.

When the phone rang that morning in Sonia's house, she could barely believe what Pedro was saying.

'Do you have anything planned for today? Can I come over in a little while? We could even go out somewhere afterwards. I have news for you. But I have to tell you in person.'

Sonia told him she had no plans for that Saturday and promised to wait for him. But in fact she did have plans. Actually, she had two plans: Faye was coming over for lunch at her place, because she wanted to talk to Andrea. A serious talk, she had said. And after lunch Andrea was going to take all the girls to the shopping centre for some shopping and a movie. But meeting Pedro took priority over all that. There was no contest.

Sonia hung up the phone, ran to the shower and called out to her two sisters, who were in the living room: 'I can't go out with you today after all. Let's leave the shopping for another time. Or you two can go without me.'

Carol looked grumpy. Going alone with her eldest sister was no fun at all, better just call it off.

But Andrea seemed pleased. 'Great!' she said. 'This way, I don't have to be stuck with you girls. Since dad has lent me the car anyway, I can take care of some stuff I want to do.'

She started getting ready as well.

As she stepped out of the shower, Sonia remembered Faye. She tried to convince Andrea to stay home for lunch and talk to Faye, but the idea wasn't met with much enthusiasm. She'd have to call Faye and cancel.

'It's OK, Sonia,' Faye said. 'Don't worry. We'll do it some other day. I'm not in a hurry anyway – this stuff happened a while ago and I've only just got the courage now to talk about it.'

There was obvious disappointment in Faye's voice, though. Sonia felt a bit guilty. Up until then, she hadn't given a second thought to whatever it was that Faye wanted to see Andrea about. It wasn't any of her business. But now she suddenly felt worried. After all, Faye and Andrea barely knew each other, they weren't the same age and they didn't hang around with the same crowd. What on earth could her friend want with her older sister?

'Are you sure it's cool?' she asked.

'Yeah,' said Faye. 'It was just some work-related stuff. Actually, I think I might call Andrea's office soon and try to meet her there. That way we can talk better.'

Hmm. That sounded bad. It was probably serious. Andrea worked in a lawyer's office, and if Faye needed to talk to her, there must be some problem.

Sonia hesitated. She didn't want to butt in. She had to respect the fact that Faye hadn't told her what it was all about. At the same time, she didn't want to leave her friend in the lurch.

'Listen, Faye, I said something came up and that's

true. But if you want I can cancel it and you can meet my sister right away. Or if you have a problem that I can help you with, just ask me. I'm your friend, and you can count on me for whatever you need. Don't forget that.'

'No, no, don't worry,' said Faye, but her tone of voice wasn't all that firm. She seemed to hesitate, but then she went on. 'I just needed to talk to her about some stuff to do with the law that I have to research. And she's the only lawyer I know. But we can do it some other time. Bye!'

And she hung up before Sonia had time to correct her and say that actually Andrea was just a law student, not a proper lawyer.

What research could Faye be talking about? She and Sonia were doing all the same subjects at school and none of the teachers had given them an essay that involved anything like that. And Faye had no intention of going to university or studying law one day. If there was anyone in Garibaldi High who had set ideas about their professional future, it was Faye-I-wanna-be-a-model. Researching stuff about the law? It didn't add up.

Sonia was just about to comment on this to her sisters when the bell rang, and Andrea looked out the window to see who was at the gate.

'It's that friend of yours, Pedro,' she said. 'He's just coming in.'

Carol started to tease Sonia. 'Ah, so *that's* why you changed your mind and decided not to hang out with us this morning, huh? Because of Pedro. Lately it's been all Pedro this, Pedro that.'

'Stop talking nonsense,' Sonia interrupted her. 'He's just come over to help me with that computer-virus thing.'

Hearing this, Andrea was suddenly interested.

'Ah, talking of viruses, you'll never guess what happened ...' and she plunged into some story about a virus at work.

Carol was giggling away ironically, to show she didn't buy her sister's excuse for this morning's visit. Sonia meanwhile had gone to open the door to Pedro. And all the time, their oldest sister was sitting in a corner of the sofa, leafing through a magazine and at the same time babbling away, describing in detail this other virus her boyfriend had told her about, even though no one was listening.

It was only when Pedro joined them in the living room that they started to take any notice of what Andrea was saying.

'It sounds very like that virus you have on your computer. Colin thinks it's a hacker, actually, and in a notary's office, you can imagine how serious that could be. Just think if someone was prying into all sorts of confidential documents. Colin kept saying we should talk to the notary public and call the police, but the office clerk was afraid of being blamed, afraid they might think he had broken something.'

Sonia and Pedro exchanged glances.

'Sorry,' Sonia said, 'what was that you were saying, Andrea? Could you say it again?' She wanted to make sure they'd got the story right.

'You don't listen when people talk and then you want them to repeat what they've said. I haven't got a replay button, you know,' said Andrea, looking a bit annoyed.

Pedro came to Sonia's defence. 'No, it was my fault. I came barging in, not realising you were in the middle of a conversation, and I started talking to her. I'm sorry.'

'All right, then,' said Andrea with a sigh. 'What I was saying was that you really need to fix that computer fast, before this virus spreads out all over the place. I think I've already contaminated Colin and he has spread it to the office. It seems to be very contagious. We could have an epidemic on our hands.'

She made it sound as if it was actually a virus or disease, spreading from one person to another.

But Pedro was interested and he had lots of questions. Andrea told them that Colin and a client had gone to sign a deed at a public notary's office, and in the middle of the document a strange sheet of paper had appeared. It seemed to be a letter, probably some sort of prank. The clerk had got all nervous, arguing with the people around him, thinking someone was trying to set him up.

'And did you keep that piece of paper?' Pedro asked. 'Or did you throw it away?'

'Which paper? The deed? It's been kept, obviously. The client took it all with him. Colin worked it out somehow and it was all fine. He's great, you know? Competent, observant –'

'No, not the *deed*. I mean the page of writing that seemed to be part of a prank.'

'Oh. I think Colin did keep it. I remember he said it might be useful.'

'And do you think he would show it to me if I asked to see it?'

Andrea was serious now. 'Of course not! Don't be silly! Professional secrecy. It's a very important rule. It's fundamental for any lawyer. This is the client's business and no one else's – it's private. Nobody can be allowed to go looking through other people's documents.' Sonia knew how distracted her sister could get. It was clear she was already thinking of something else, talking and reading the magazine at the same time. She'd better make it very clear.

'No, Andrea, nobody wants to look at any client's documents. Pedro just wants to see the prank letter to study the virus. It's just a technical curiosity. Maybe it will help him to fix my computer. Perhaps you could give him Colin's number? Then they can talk directly.'

Andrea agreed and gave Pedro Colin's number.

Sonia grabbed her backpack and, within moments, Andrea was back reading her magazine as Sonia and Pedro left the room.

Pedro was very excited by what he had just heard.

'The Brainy Hacker strikes again,' he said. 'It's all becoming clearer. As soon as I heard, I came over to tell you.'

'As soon as you heard? But Andrea only just told us the story, so how could you have known it already?'

'I didn't know that part, of course. No, I mean, there's been a new attack. What I came to tell you was about what happened on Will's computer. Apparently it was a double attack this time.'

Though, actually, it was a triple attack, but at this stage they had no idea that Faye was having similar experiences.

Perhaps even quadruple. But they had even less of an inkling about Robbie's misfortunes. It would be weeks before they would hear about that.

6 – A Matter of Strategy

Will was crazy about games – any games. He'd even play cards or do jigsaw puzzles, whatever was to hand. But, no question about it, his favourite kind were electronic games. If he could, he would spend twenty-four hours a day gaming – chasing, escaping, scoring, levelling up, planning gameplays, beating records. To him, a TV set or a computer were just peripherals to a gaming console.

Will didn't watch sitcoms, he didn't watch the news, he didn't care about the music videos everyone liked to keep up with, except for the occasional heavy metal band. He turned on the TV only to watch sport – any kind of sport. Football, basketball, volleyball, even chess, snooker and golf, when they got this stuff on cable. Matt swore that one day he actually caught Will watching a domino championship, though Will insisted that was just a joke.

But it was no joke that Will hardly ever spent any time on the internet or chatting with friends online. Most of the time, he was disconnected from the world, playing for hours on end. His favourite games were the ones you could play online with friends and that go on for ever, throwing little dice, playing the role of heroes or villains, alternating between tense silences and loud yells.

The others always thought it would be hard to beat Will, with all that practice he had. He had fast reflexes. That's why his friends didn't like playing action games against him. It was no fun any more, because he always won. It didn't matter whether they were using a controller, a mouse or a keyboard. Will was just a winner.

The one exception was strategy games. Will was not all that good at games like that, especially at the more advanced stages. He didn't have a lot of patience. So he'd often get a friend to come over to his place to help him out with the planning, so that he could learn and improve his skills. Someone like Pedro, for instance, who was the kind of person that could stay silent for a long time, analysing the alternatives for a game he was imagining, a game he hadn't even started to play yet, that only existed in his head.

Pedro would sometimes interrupt the game, leave the room, make a sandwich, come back eating it, and all the time he would be thinking about his next move. And, in the end, it usually worked.

It was exciting to have a strong opponent every once in a while. So Will sometimes liked to play against Pedro, each in his own house, on different computers. At other times, though, they would just sit down side by side, playing together against the computer. At times like that, Pedro was invaluable. He really improved the chances of winning. And it was at one of these times that the Brainy Hacker decided to strike again.

The two friends were playing a new game, full of different obstacles. It was on a CD that Will's godfather had brought back to him from a trip to London. It was set in the Middle Ages, Will's favourite era, and was full of knights, armour, castles, sieges, jousting, tournaments with flags that waved in the wind, damsels locked in towers, magic potions, dragons, Crusades, illuminated parchments, wizards, spells, dungeons. Loads of stuff. You could play for hours, always with new elements, without it ever becoming repetitive.

That's why Pedro went on playing for a while, then a little while longer, and ended up spending the whole of Friday afternoon and evening at Will's place. And that's how he happened to see a message that appeared all of a sudden on the screen, totally out of the blue.

Will was just about to delete it, but Pedro intervened to keep the message on the screen for a few minutes – long enough to read it a couple of times before it all disappeared, when the impatient

Will made a quick and unstoppable movement that brought the game back to the main screen.

'I can't say I memorised it, but I did pay close attention and I think I can roughly repeat it,' Pedro was saying to Sonia now, as they walked to Will's house that Saturday morning.

Well, Sonia thought, he hadn't exactly called her up for a Saturday date with a movie and a bite to eat, as she had dared to imagine, full of hope. Still, it was clear that he wanted her company and valued her help in this challenge of trying to track down the hacker.

'Do you really think it was a new attack from the virus? Or by the Brainy Hacker?'

'Yes, I do. But Will is sure that it couldn't be, because the game was on a commercial CD and it's a closed system. You can't add stuff into it. The game doesn't have an online mode and it can't receive messages via the web.'

He paused and then said, 'Only, when we played it, it did look as if it was able to pick up stuff from somewhere else. I'm sure the Brainy Hacker did use the monitor, but this time the message couldn't have come over the internet. It came through the game itself. It's much the same as what happened the other times, except that this time the hacker used a character.'

'What do you mean?' asked Sonia curiously. They

had almost arrived at Will's gate by this time, and they had decided to try and repeat the experience. At least, that was the idea.

As they walked, Pedro had been explaining that there were loads of characters in this game. Depending on the situation, a player could be harmed by one of the characters, and that meant he or she would forfeit some items, for instance. But a player could also win points, of course, or get help from allies to face a challenge. These allies could be warriors, or a knight maybe, or a wizard. And the place where the mysterious message had appeared, that time when Will and Pedro were playing, was in a tower belonging to one of these wizard characters.

'A wizard! Like, with a boiling cauldron, a pointy hat, a starry cape?' asked Sonia, surprised. 'Will likes playing with stuff like that?'

Pedro pretended to be concentrating on opening the gate, but really he was hesitating, wondering how to answer. He wanted Sonia to take the game seriously, to see it as a grown-up thing, not some silly kids' stuff. He certainly didn't want her asking Will questions like that.

After a few seconds' thought, he answered: 'You don't want to take much notice of those things, Sonia. These games are all like that, with wizards and magic and stuff, but it's just a set. They're actually very sophisticated and difficult. Complex as chess, for example. They require intelligence, highly developed logical thinking –'

'And a blue cape covered in little stars?' Sonia chipped in with a smile.

'No, I can't say I saw a cape,' said Pedro seriously. 'In the game, we were inside a castle. The wizard wasn't about to go outside – he was in the tower. Maybe he just wears a cape in bad weather, who knows? But yes, there was a cauldron. And a pointy hat. And a lot of glass bottles with colourful liquids bubbling in them. There was an owl perched in a corner. And a big book.'

'Full of recipes for spells?' she went on, teasing him. 'And was there a magic wand?'

She was really quite surprised at all this childish stuff in Will's game. He had always seemed such a dark kind of guy. He wore black and listened to punk and heavy metal bands. He always put on such grown-up airs – and now suddenly she finds out he's into fairy tales, the kind of thing that she and her girlfriends had left behind ages ago.

Pedro replied, slightly impatiently, 'How am I supposed to know? I didn't go flicking through the book. It was on a screen, remember? But listen, suddenly the book spun around, changed position and faced us, wide open and showing the pages – and there was this message written on it. So, tell me, are you still very interested in the details of the costumes and décor, or can I tell you what we read on that screen, on those pages?'

He sounded annoyed.

'No, I'm sorry, go ahead. What was written on the book? Tell me!'

But just at that moment, Will's mother opened the door and invited them in, all smiles. A few minutes of polite small talk followed, so it was some time before the three friends were together at the computer, and Sonia asked again, 'So, go on, tell me, what was this mysterious message you got?'

'Well,' said Pedro, 'it was in those weird fancy letters, with the first letter on the page written very big and surrounded by all these detailed illustrations in gold and red and blue.'

'Gothic,' said Will, the medieval expert. 'That kind of writing is called gothic script. And the way the first letter on a page is all coloured and illustrated – that's called an illuminated initial.'

'But what did it *say*?' Sonia asked.

'It started with two sentences that I remember exactly,' said Pedro. '"To you I will tell it. I am not who everyone thinks I am."'

'*Cool!*' said Sonia. 'A mysterious character. But it could easily be part of the game. If nobody can hack into a CD, then the message must already have been part of it, no?'

Will spoke then. 'I thought the same, at first, but we soon saw that it couldn't be.'

'That was what I thought too,' Pedro went on. 'But the very next thing in the message was an apology for butting into our game and interrupting what we were doing. The message explained that there was no other way, because they needed to communicate with us and simply using the internet wasn't working.'

'That made us realise it couldn't be part of the game,' Will interrupted. 'I mean, come on, like anyone would talk about the internet in a medieval game? So I wanted to close it down and get on with the game, but Pedro wouldn't let me. And then this whole stream of other letters started appearing like mad, page after page. The guy was telling this big long story, and he wouldn't let us play on.'

The boys told Sonia that the message's mysterious author introduced himself, saying that he wasn't actually the wizard they had seen in the game moments before. He was just an assistant who was still learning the secrets of alchemy. But he studied a lot, and he could read and write and knew Latin.

'He was explaining the whole time that he could read well and quickly,' said Will. 'He said that he was used to reading, that he had studied in some monastery, but that at that time almost everyone was illiterate.'

'The Brainy Hacker always says stuff like that,' said Sonia, as if she were talking about an old friend. 'And then?'

'Then he said that a long, long time before, on a day on which the wizard was performing one of his experiments looking for the Elixir of Youth, there was a little accident.'

'Wait a minute,' said Sonia. 'This elixir – what's that? I thought alchemy was about the Philosopher's Stone?'

'Yes, that's right,' said Will. 'The Philosopher's Stone was a mysterious substance that could turn everything it touched into gold, and it was a stone, of course.'

'Hence the name,' Sonia added with a grin.

'Yes,' Will went on, 'and the alchemists were always experimenting to see if they could find the powerful substance of which this stone was made. They hoped that one day someone might find the stone among some treasures in the East or something. But the other thing they were interested in finding was the Elixir of Youth, which was a liquid. The Stone and the Elixir were different things, but some scholars believed that the discovery of the Stone would be a first step towards finding the Elixir. Among the aims of alchemy were the discovery of the Stone and the Elixir, and also other things, such as the Machine of Perpetual Motion.'

Sonia was beginning to be sorry she'd asked. She hadn't really wanted a lecture on alchemy.

Alchemy was not very highly thought of any more, Will said, but in fact the alchemists of old had done a lot of important research. The search for perpetual motion had ended up helping to develop physics. The search for the Elixir of Youth and the Philosopher's Stone had contributed to findings in chemistry. So it wasn't just silly magic, like a lot of people think. Deep down, the paths of humanity ...

That's enough! thought Pedro. He really felt like screaming at Will to stop. But he didn't want to be mean to his friend. So he just said, 'I'm sorry, but aren't we straying a bit from the subject here, Will?'

'Oh,' said Will. 'I didn't realise. I was just explaining how this alchemy thing worked in the Middle Ages, so Sonia could understand the message from the wizard's assistant.'

'Yeah, OK, but now you've explained it, everybody gets it. Can we move on?'

Will nodded, slightly offended, and let Pedro carry on. So Pedro explained what the wizard's assistant had told them.

One time, while the wizard was doing some experiment, a few drops of liquid had splashed over the assistant. It was just a little accident, but those few drops had consequences, and the effects endured over time.

'That Elixir of Youth thing?' Sonia asked. 'So he got baby skin in a few parts of his body, where the liquid touched him, maybe?' She was trying to imagine what that would look like.

'No,' Will said. 'This liquid was probably not the Elixir of Youth, or of Eternal Life, as it was sometimes called. In fact, it couldn't have been, because the elixir was never found. With the passing years, even the alchemists started believing that it couldn't ever be developed. They gave up looking for it. Later, only the explorers kept looking for the Fountain of Youth in distant lands.'

'But anyway,' Pedro picked up the story, 'what our guy said, the wizard's assistant, was that what splashed on him was this liquid that was being experimented with. It wasn't the Elixir of Youth itself, but it was maybe going to be an ingredient in the elixir.

'And it didn't affect his skin, as you imagined it might, Sonia, but it had consequences in his spirit. Something deeper than an effect on the surface of the body.'

'What on earth do you mean?' asked Sonia.

'Well, from what this person told us, something in him never died. He may not have gained eternal youth, but he did gain a kind of eternal life, a sort of immortality, I don't exactly know, but something like that.'

'So the guy's a zombie?' squawked Sonia. 'Like, the living dead?'

'No,' said Pedro. 'As Will explained, it's not his *body* that lives for ever, it's not physical eternity. It's his spirit that goes on living for ever.'

Sonia came up in goosebumps at that thought.

Pedro continued: 'Something mental, it appears to be. But he wasn't able to explain this thing properly, whatever it was. So that's what we want to find out.'

'Exactly!' Will was getting excited. 'So the plan is, we'll play the game again until we get to the same point, in the same room, and then we can see if the big alchemy book turns towards us again with another message.'

'Or at least with a ready-made chemistry project,' joked Sonia. She was feeling a bit nervous, and she was trying to cover up. 'We have to hand in our paper to Ms Nancy next week, remember? Just as Matt suggested back on that very first day, when Mr Costa gave us such a good grade for our history project.'

But the boys didn't find this very funny, so Sonia decided to keep her mouth shut from now on.

They tried for hours, the three of them in front of the computer monitor. They overcame many obstacles. They came to the tower of the wizard with his pointy hat – without any stars or magic wand. But this time the wizard's assistant did not show up.

It was a huge disappointment. They had all been

sure that something was going to happen, but nothing did.

The day would have been a total waste, only that when she arrived home that night Sonia found a printed sheet of paper on the desk, next to a brief note in Andrea's handwriting.

Unfortunately, Pedro was no longer with her. They had said goodbye outside her building and he had already left. And he had no mobile phone.

Sonia read what was written on the two pieces of paper over and over again while she waited for Pedro to get home so that she could talk to him on the landline.

The note from Andrea said:

Sonia,
I talked to Colin and he sent this copy of the contaminated message for Pedro. Anyway, he wants Pedro to call him, because he also wants to investigate this computer virus thing.
All the best,
Andrea

On the other sheet was a much longer message. Sonia read it once, then she read it again, paying close attention.

She closed her eyes to think. The language it used

was so weird, some bits were hard to understand. She really needed to read it more than twice.

Trading the safety of the closed seas for the amplitude of the surrounding ocean, after a few nights we started to perceive the Polar Star drowning in the horizon. After maintaining the course for a few days further, I reached for the first time your gracious lands. Others had already arrived in these parts, and about their finds I had read extensively. But none such reading had prepared this notary for the beauty of your coast, reaching wide as far as the eye could see. Nor for the great barriers it boasts along the sea in some parts – sometimes white, others red, with the earth above covered by trees – nor for its white beaches, ripe with tall palm trees and infinite waters.

I appreciated it so and learned to admire the loveliness and goodness of your people with such strength that I continued to visit you throughout the centuries, even if rarely noticed by anyone. Or, on the rare occasion in which such a risk occurred, I have always succeeded so that the encounter presented itself as a dream, delirium or fantasy, as was required of my difficult condition. It has only been in these more recent times, faced with the unexpected possibilities of what you call the 'new technologies', that I have occasionally succumbed to the temptation of breaking the ropes that bind me and making rapid visits to some of you, with much caution and prudence.

In previous times, the captain of a vessel would occasionally order a few of their crew to descend among the inhabitants of the land, to note how they lived and discover from them all that could be discovered, even if the languages spoken were not the same. I feel now as if I am acting as such.

Today, however, as I perceived in your writings a reference to the job of notary, I came to the realisation that we are brothers in office, and that this may per fortune bring us together. If such a thing comes to occur, this notary officer, now a Christian, will find immense satisfaction on the path to redemption, and shall pray in grace to the Lord Our Saviour, who commences to free him of his millennial condemnation.

Vasco Manoel Coutinho

Pedro listened while Sonia read him the message over the phone.

When she had finished, all he said was, 'Wow! Could you read it again, please?'

So she read it again, and by now Pedro was really interested.

'That's mad! Another one! And it's signed! He says he's a notary – some kind of lawyer, I suppose. It sounds like he's one of the first Europeans to discover the Americas, don't you think? That stuff about "your gracious lands"?'

'That's what I thought,' said Sonia, 'but then there's all that other stuff about computers and so on. Weird.'

'With so many messages coming, our man's got to have slipped up some time; we just need to find out when and where.'

'But how do we do that?'

'I don't know, Sonia. But we have to find a clue. I'm not going to ask you to read it again, that'd be a bit much. But I'm really starting to feel that we're going to be able to work this out.'

'Do you have a fax machine at home?' asked Sonia. 'Because I could fax it to you and then you can read it as many times as you like.'

'No, I don't. But why don't you just scan it and email it to me.'

'We haven't got a scanner here. I could scan it in my dad's office, but not until Monday.'

'That's no use. If we have to wait until Monday, you might as well give it to me yourself at school.'

The message wasn't all that long, Sonia thought. She could type it up and email it to him.

She was just about to say that, when Pedro said, 'I think I'll come over to your place tomorrow and take a look. Would that be OK? Or are you sick of me after spending a whole Saturday together?'

Was it OK? Of course it was! Two days in a row with Pedro all to herself, and at the weekend too. She really seemed to be in luck. In a way, the Brainy Hacker was playing Cupid. These pranks were helping to bring Pedro close to her.

'Yeah, that's all right,' she said, trying not to sound too enthusiastic. 'That way, we can compare all the stuff we've already got from this guy, and we'll definitely come up with a clue. It's just a matter of strategy.'

And of luck, she thought. *Lots of luck.*

7 – Message in a Bottle

Sonia and Pedro spent a good part of Sunday morning organising the information they already had about the Brainy Hacker. They not only worked on what he (or she) had left by way of the weird messages, but they also made a summary of what they remembered from the other appearance that hadn't left a printed record. They read it all over and over and made lots of notes, using up piles of scrap paper.

They only interrupted their work for lunch, which was a fantastic Sunday spaghetti dish cooked by Sonia's Italian grandmother. The tomato sauce had been left cooking over a low heat since morning, filling the house with a tempting smell that made it harder and harder for the kids to concentrate as the clock moved forward and their stomachs told them it was time to eat.

'You're staying to lunch with us, Pedro, right?' said Mrs D'Angelo hospitably. 'I'm going to set an extra place at the table.'

'Nonna's food is amazing,' said Sonia.

There was no need to insist. Pedro had heard of her famous spaghetti, even though he'd never tasted it. And the delicious smell was irresistible.

'I didn't tell my mum I was staying out for lunch,' said Pedro. 'But yes, I'll stay, thank you. I just need to phone home and let them know.'

When he hung up the phone, he asked, 'Is it alright if I use your phone again? My mum says there's an urgent message for me. Apparently, Matt has called my house three times already. If he has spent his Sunday morning calling me, something must have happened.'

Something certainly had. A new attack from the Brainy Hacker.

By now, almost all the friends had been exchanging ideas and impressions about the joker's activities. All except for Faye, who was too scatterbrained (or at least that's what they all thought), and Matt, who had heard all the stories but never had anything to tell. To be honest, he was starting to feel a bit jealous that nobody had sent him any mysterious messages. He was also slightly anxious that his friends would start thinking he might be to blame for what was happening. After all, if he was the only one who wasn't getting these weird messages, that made him a natural suspect.

That was why he got so excited when he joined the club: he had finally got a message. This was what he wanted to tell Pedro so urgently, why he'd made all those phone calls, as the other two soon found out.

'Now the guy says he's a priest, Pedro! Can you imagine?'

'No, I can't imagine,' answered Pedro. 'You couldn't make this stuff up. Did you manage to print out the message?'

'Of course!' said Matt. 'After everything you have been saying, how could I let this pass? I printed everything out. I've got the page right here in my hand. Want me to read it out for you?'

'Yes.'

Matt read it, and then Pedro asked Matt to email the document to him.

By now, Carol had got interested in all this as well. It really bugged Sonia, but her younger sister wouldn't go away, so there the three of them were, all curiosity, standing around the computer. Sure enough, the message came through, and soon they were reading on the screen:

Although you have an evangelist's name, you do not seem to apply yourself much to the written word, which is a shame. Especially during an epoch in which there is such ease to learn to read.

There were times when almost all people in a society were illiterate. Only a few had access to written pages. Books were rare and precious, and none but the very rich could afford to own them. It is no wonder that it was so, as each volume demanded painstaking and intensive work from all of us, who dedicated ourselves to copying so that the texts could multiply and perpetuate themselves.

In the West, in monasteries such as the one where my companions and I worked in our scriptorium in teams of five at a time, only the Church and the universities could claim to gather people skilled in reading and writing. Even kings and emperors were illiterate.

Fortunately, I had the opportunity, years later, to experience different realities. Even when fate brought me to your continent centuries later, as a member of the Jesuit company, so many among us had this skill that we even managed to assemble a small compilation of the vocabulary of the peoples found on these shores.

The written word of some of my companions managed to reach a larger extension, to go beyond the immediate surroundings and the people who were close to them and defend poor locations from the cruelty and evildoings of those who thought only of enslaving them, as if they were not human and had no soul. In a way, this written word had an effect, by influencing our society so that it would not accept that the peoples found in the New World were reduced to captivity and treated as animals.

However, such protection ultimately directed the cruelty to other peoples, and the sad fate of slavery fell upon the shoulders of our African brothers, who were for centuries victims of this atrocity.

Therefore, one cannot help observing that humanity only walks in slow and short steps, on a path with abundant setbacks and detours. Even if sometimes one has the impression that there have been improvements, we are soon obliged to note melancholically that there are other aspects to consider.

At any rate, it seems doubtless that without the transmission of wisdom and knowledge from other generations through the art of the written word, our situation would look grimmer still. Each individual would be forced to start from the beginning and reinvent it all. And Our Lord's work would move in circles, condemned to repetition throughout the centuries, as the pagans would tell with the story of poor Sisyphus.

As this poor scribe who, try as he might, can never succeed in finding a kind soul to free him from his sorrows, woe is me!

It ended just like that. Suddenly. No goodbyes. They rang Matt again, asking if there was anything missing. There wasn't, he said. But he couldn't contain his excitement any more and wanted to meet them.

'Can I come over?' he pleaded.

Of course he could. Soon they were all gathered, rereading the printouts of the message that Matt brought for everyone.

'Hey, you know what? There's something new here!' said Pedro, as he finished reading the message again.

'What's that?' asked Matt. 'Do you know this priest?'

'No, that's not it. But look: he repeats a lot of the stuff he already said before, in the other messages. He makes a big deal about writing, says he's all proud that he's one of the few who knew how to read and write, stuff like that.'

'He always says that,' Sonya interjected. 'That's not new, Pedro.'

'No, you're right, that's not the new bit.'

She did like Pedro, but sometimes she wished he didn't have to go round and round when he was talking. She sighed inwardly and waited.

'What's different this time is that he is quite clear about living in different centuries. See, in the second paragraph, he says "in monasteries such as the one where my companions and I worked in our scriptorium ..." A scriptorium is where medieval monks made their manuscripts, so that's the Middle Ages, right?'

The others nodded.

'And then, look, later it says, "Even when fate brought me to your continent, centuries later, as a member of the Jesuit company ... " So now he's a Jesuit missionary to the Americas, and he even says "centuries later". That's what's new, Sonia. He is specifically saying he has lived in different times. It's a bit like what the wizard's assistant was saying before, but this time it's much clearer.'

Sonia had to agree.

'What about this Sisyphus person?' asked Matt. 'Do you know anything about him?'

'I do,' said Sonia. 'I've heard of him. My grandpa was talking about him the other day. It's a Greek myth, I think, and it's about a man who was condemned to push a huge rock uphill for all eternity. I don't know why, but I remember that as soon as he arrived on the top and stopped to rest, the rock would roll downhill and he had to do it all over again.'

'Listen, Matt,' Pedro said. 'Before I talked to you, Sonia and I were making a list of the things that we have gathered from all the messages.'

'Show him the list,' suggested Sonia, and they showed it to him.

- It's someone who's proud of knowing how to read and write.
- It's set in a different place and time in each message.

- His grammar is pretty mixed up.
- He writes in an old-fashioned style, but the text arrives by computer.
- Changes sex.

'Wait, I don't get it,' said Matt. 'What do you mean, "changes sex"?'

'Oh, yeah, right, we didn't explain that,' said Sonia. 'What we meant was that sometimes the hacker says they're a woman: an Egyptian queen, a merchant's wife, whatever ... But at other times they write as if they're a man.'

'This priest, or the notary from the ship, for instance,' Pedro recalled. 'Or the alchemist's assistant. And Marco Polo.'

'What assistant?' asked Matt, feeling a bit left out of secrets the others seemed to be in on. 'What alchemist? What notary? What are you talking about?'

'You should explain it to him properly,' said Carol. 'You can't expect him to guess!'

She was right, of course. A lot of the messages Pedro had mentioned were very recent. They'd only come in over the weekend. He and Sonia hadn't had a chance to tell the others yet.

'Well, the alchemist's assistant is this wizard who appeared in the middle of Will's computer game and started writing on the screen, but he didn't leave a written message, because Will closed it,' Pedro began. 'The notary guy is new too – we only heard from him last night.'

Matt was obviously putting all the pieces together in his head as he read the messages and listened to what Sonia and Pedro were telling him, and at last he said, 'I think we can add something to that list of yours.'

'What?' asked the other two together.

'I'm not exactly sure – I can't explain it properly. But I get the impression this guy's asking for help. And I feel like helping him.'

'Help?' asked Sonia, puzzled. 'Who? The hacker? You mean this person wants to turn us into accomplices or something?'

'Hey, listen,' said Pedro, 'hacking into other people's computers is a crime: we could go to jail for that. You can count me out.'

Matt didn't know what they were talking about.

'I'll tell you what I'm thinking,' said Pedro. 'This is clearly not a virus, but a hacker, right?'

Matt agreed that it did look like that.

'We're dealing with someone smart and competent,' said Pedro, 'someone who's really good with computers, someone who knows his history and uses that as a kind of disguise. He changes what he says depending on who he's talking to. He moves from ancient Egypt to Babylon to Medieval times to the time of the explorers, and so on. And he or she takes on the character of a queen, an alchemist, a scribe, a priest, a merchant ... '

'We think this person knows us pretty well,' Sonia added, 'because he is able to pick up on what we are thinking or working on.'

'This last message to you, Matt,' said Pedro, 'mentions your name being the same as one of the Evangelists. Those were the people who wrote the gospels, and one of them was Matthew. That's pretty personal, right? This guy really does know us.'

'Or he can read thoughts,' suggested Carol, but nobody took any notice of her.

Pedro continued. 'These weird messages look like some kind of joke or game. But it may not be a game at all. The way I see it, this is a way of marking territory, of showing that someone has been there and has left a trail. That's what hackers do. We still don't know who it is, or why they're doing it, or why we were chosen – or if perhaps this is happening also to other people out there, but we haven't heard about it.

'The thing is, this might be serious. And I hate to keep saying this, but hacking is a crime, and I really don't like the idea of getting mixed up with a hacker.'

The others stayed silent, thinking.

'I mean,' Pedro went on after a while, 'what if the guy breaks into a bank system and steals a load of money? Or hacks into some government stuff, destroys a security system? He could do anything. Stuff we can't even imagine. People could get hurt, you know?'

Sonia got goosebumps all over again. Feeling a bit awkward, she made a suggestion. 'Should we maybe tell the police? Instead of trying to figure this out ourselves.'

'I'm not sure about that,' Pedro said hesitantly. 'They might not take us seriously. I mean, it does sound very weird. They might just laugh at us.'

Sonia nodded. Very likely.

'But, listen, I have another idea,' Pedro said. 'I thought of maybe talking to Colin and showing him everything. He's experienced – he's a lawyer – so maybe he could help us out, give us a few tips.'

'Who is this Colin?' asked Matt.

'That lawyer who's dating Sonia's sister. He's the one who sent us a copy of the message that a clerk in their office found, all mixed up with a legal document. Actually, he left a message for us, saying he wanted to have a chat about it. I'd forgotten that.'

Matt thought it over. 'Yes ...' he said hesitantly. 'I suppose.' But he did not seem convinced.

He thought a bit more and then he said, 'What if it's not that at all?'

'What do you mean?' asked Sonia. 'Not what?'

'Do you have a better suggestion?' said Pedro.

'No,' said Matt. 'I can't say I have a suggestion or that it's any better than your ideas. But I just keep thinking it may not be a hacker or a criminal or anything like that. Maybe it's just a cry for help. Like this is someone who needs help and has been gradually trying to gain our confidence, to make friends with us.'

'Yeah, right, so they can use us later!' said Sonia.

'I don't think so,' said Matt. 'I don't see any sign of that. I think this person is trying to get to know us so that he or she can open up and tell us what they want. I honestly don't see them using us. In fact, I think it's the other way round – we're the ones who used that first message to get a good grade on the history paper.

'And by the way, we'd definitely lose that grade in a second if we went around telling people that the famous project that got all those compliments from Mr Costa wasn't done by us, but was actually plagiarised from Nefertiti or somebody else who sent us everything ready-made and full of details.'

Silence.

'See, I read these messages quite differently,' Matt went on. 'I mean, I do agree with all that stuff you two wrote in your list: it's someone who's proud of knowing how to read and write, who has lived in different places and through different times and all that. But I also see someone who is polite, who apologises for butting in, who treats us with respect.

And it's someone who's really hooked on this idea of how important it is to study.'

'That's right,' Sonia agreed.

'But it's also someone who's trying to communicate,' Matt said. 'Desperately trying, actually, in any way and over a long time. Someone who sends one message after another. Someone who says they are suffering, who needs to be set free from some kind of a sentence. Someone who hopes that we can give them a little help. And what is our response? We couldn't care less. Or worse: we think they're a criminal.'

Silence again.

Pedro and Sonia hadn't seen things from that angle. They remained quiet, thinking. Since thoughts don't make noise, there was no sound to be heard.

The person who finally spoke was Carol. They had all forgotten she was there. She was usually very nosy, but on this occasion she'd really been trying to control herself and not ask too many questions, so she wouldn't get kicked out by the older kids.

It was Carol, though, who summed up the situation, saying, 'Cool! It's a bit like a message in a bottle, like you see in cartoons, floating in the middle of the waves until it reaches a beach and someone opens it. And we are the ones opening it, right?'

What if this were true?

8 – Model What?

They managed to make an appointment with Colin for the following day, in his office. They would stop by in the afternoon, they'd said, all three of them, because Matt was constantly stuck to the other two now.

Sonia thanked her lucky stars that she had managed at least to get rid of Carol, who loved Colin and had tried to tag along with the group. But that would have been a bit much. She wasn't in their class and Sonia felt that having one sister hanging around this meeting was more than enough.

That was Andrea, of course, who worked with Colin. Andrea greeted the three kids with a complaint that none of them understood: 'You can't manage to arrive on time even for important meetings, huh?' she said as soon as they arrived. And then she was gone, disappearing through the door, leaving the others in the waiting room outside the office.

They couldn't imagine what she was talking about. They weren't late. In fact, they had been so excited about the meeting with Colin that they had arrived more than twenty minutes early. What on earth did Andrea mean, telling them off like that for being late?

The three friends stayed sitting in the waiting area, flicking through old magazines and hearing the receptionist answer one phone call after another. It was only when Andrea opened the door again and gestured for someone to leave the other room that Sonia realised what had happened. The person who was leaving the office was Faye.

And Andrea was saying, 'I thought you were all together. I just assumed you were here for that earlier meeting. What a coincidence – everybody coming over on the same day.'

So that explained why Andrea had thought they were late! Faye had made an appointment just before the others were due to meet Colin. And Andrea, who was always a bit scatty, obviously thought it was all the same meeting. Faye sat down to chat with Matt and Pedro and Sonia.

'So, did you manage to sort out whatever it was that you had to discuss with Andrea?' Sonia asked.

'Yes, I did get some advice from her on this contract I needed to have looked over, but then I was telling her this other stuff, and then Colin came in and heard what I was saying. He seemed to find it interesting, and next thing he suggested I should stay for this meeting he's having with you lot.'

Sonia looked at Matt and Pedro. Why would

Colin invite Faye to join in their meeting? Not that they minded, of course, she was their friend, but it seemed a bit odd.

'So, anyway, Andrea and I talked over this contract a bit more and –'

'What contract?' asked Matt, interrupting so suddenly that Sonia was startled.

Faye looked at him and gave a bright smile that lit up her beautiful face. Her hair was so soft and silky that it looked like it belonged in a shampoo ad. All that was missing was the slow-motion camera and some classical music playing in the background. At least, that was more or less how Matt always thought about Faye.

Matt was living with a permanent dilemma: either he should put Faye out of his mind once and for all (because he knew she was so gorgeous that she was way out of his league), or he should not forget about her even for a minute for the rest of his life (because he couldn't even if he tried, because she was the most special person he had ever met, or simply just because ...).

And now, here she was, all of a sudden, right in front of him, unexpectedly, and outside class hours. A total surprise.

He listened as she explained, in her soft voice. 'Well, as you're all aware, I've always known what I wanted for my future: I –'

'Wanna-be-a-model!' The other two finished her sentence.

This was an ongoing joke in their class. Matt didn't find it so funny. But Faye had a good sense of humour and smiled. That smile. Again!

'That's right! I want to be a model. It's always been my dream.'

Nothing new so far. But then came something the others didn't know.

'Right, but then something happened, see? A few days ago, I was coming out of this shop and a woman approached me. Such a coincidence: she said she had been watching me for a few minutes, she thought I looked interesting and decided to ask if I would be up for doing a modelling audition, and if I had ever thought of anything like that.'

It would make more sense to ask if she had ever thought of anything else, thought Pedro. But he didn't interrupt.

'Then the woman said I should take some pictures and make a book and that she would help me –'

'You want to be careful with these things,' Matt cut in. 'It could be a scam. There's this stuff in the news all the time. They have criminal organisations that specialise in recruiting girls to exploit.'

Faye shook her head, but Matt was really on a roll now.

'They even kidnap girls,' he was saying now, 'then they take them abroad, make them do all sorts of horrible things. They keep promising work, fame, money, but it's just exploitation. You shouldn't trust these people, Faye. I think you should report this to the police.'

'Oh, Matt, you're so sweet. It's great having a friend like you who cares about me and watches out for me.'

Ah, the flicker of those beautiful eyelashes made him melt on the inside. And that lovely smile. And her voice that carried on, soft but firm.

'But there's no need to worry, Matt, I wasn't born yesterday. Since I've always wanted to be a model, my parents have warned me about all that stuff. I would never follow up this kind of contact without talking to them first.'

'Good,' said Matt, relieved.

'I didn't give her my number. See? I know the rules! And later I got my dad to ring *her*. But I love seeing that you're an angel who cares for me.'

(Love? Angel? He was almost dizzy.)

'Anyway,' Faye continued, 'the woman made a couple of proposals and a few days later she sent the draft of a contract for us to look over.'

Matt nodded.

'There were lots of technical terms in it, though. My parents said that it seemed cool, but they're not experts, so we thought it would be good to get a lawyer to look it over. But that's expensive, so when

I remembered your sister is in law school, Sonia, I thought I might ask her to take a look. That's all.'

So that was it. That's why Faye had this mysterious need to talk to Andrea to discuss legal stuff. One mystery solved.

'But you know what?' said Pedro. 'I don't get why Colin wanted you to stay on for the meeting with us. We're here to talk to him about this virus that has been appearing in some of our computers lately. Or it could be a hacker, who knows, someone who invades people's inboxes with weird messages and nobody knows where they're from.'

'The same one from the history project?' asked Faye.

'That's the one.'

'Ah, so that's why, of course ... I get it now. See, remember I said how Colin came into the office when I was telling Andrea about something that happened to me, something a bit like that, actually, and he overheard me.'

'*What?* A bit like what? Have you been getting messages too?'

This was new!

'Yeah, I was telling Andrea about these weird messages I've been getting.'

Pedro took a deep breath and asked, very calmly, 'Could you please explain, Faye? This could be important.'

'Well, it all started with some text messages ..'

Matt, on the other hand, wasn't calm at all. First, he had just discovered that Faye let herself get approached by random people when she left shops, just like that, people who could drag her halfway across the world and take her far away from the classrooms at Garibaldi High. Never again that smile, that dark, shiny hair, those long eyelashes that blinked slowly as if they were dancing in slow motion. And now it seemed the girl was getting strange text messages. They could be dangerous! Threatening, perhaps. In any case, they seemed to bother these lawyers, and these were people who were experienced in dealing with criminals and felons.

But he shouldn't really be surprised. Of course, the whole world was probably dying to send text messages to Faye's mobile, to ask her out or simply to tell her how beautiful she was. Not everyone was like him, too embarrassed to say how he felt. What if she accepted one of these invitations?

'What did these texts say?' he asked.

'The first one didn't really say anything, it just asked a question.'

'Well, what did it *ask*, then?'

'"What is this book that you want so badly?"'

'I don't get it,' said Pedro.

'Me neither,' said Sonia. 'We didn't ask for any book.'

Faye smiled. Smiled! And said, 'Right, I didn't get it either for a moment. There was no number, no identification, I didn't know where it was sent from or who was asking. Or what book they were talking about. Not at first.'

'But *why* were they asking about a book?' asked Sonia. 'Were you at a bookstore and some guy wanted to approach you with a gift?'

Bless her. That's exactly what Matt had been wanting to ask, but he couldn't even set his thoughts in order.

'No, not at all. Actually, I was at home, alone, locked in my room, dancing and singing that I was going to make my modelling portfolio.'

'You dance alone locked in your room?' repeated Matt, trying to picture the scene.

Sonia cut in. 'Of course, Matt, everyone does that. In front of the mirror. Especially when we're happy and we know that nobody's watching. Are you saying you never dance with happiness?'

Matt suddenly felt like an alien from a different planet because he had never in his whole life stayed alone in his room, dancing in front of the mirror.

'I don't dance either,' protested Pedro, coming to Matt's rescue.

'Well, I do,' Sonia assured them.

It was probably a girl thing. Come to think of it, Matt remembered seeing his sister dancing alone at home more than once, though she wasn't locked in her room at the time.

Pedro brought them back to the subject. 'Go on, Faye. So, you were dancing alone, you heard the phone beep, it was a text message asking which book you wanted ...'

'That's right. And of course I didn't get it right away. But then I realised what it meant.'

'And what was it?' The question came from all three, almost at the same time.

Colin came into the waiting room just at that moment. But when he saw that they were deep in conversation, he gestured to them to carry on talking, indicating that he didn't want to interrupt.

Faye went on explaining, all practical now. This side to Faye sometimes caught her friends off-guard, because she was usually pretty vague.

'Obviously, somebody must have heard what I was singing, someone who knew that I was excited about getting my book done – my modelling book, that is. It's someone who must live on another planet, because they don't even know that a model's book is her picture portfolio. Nowadays, everybody knows that: it's in the newspapers, in magazines, on reality TV shows.'

It was an intelligent enough deduction. Except for two details. The first was that not everybody lives in this world of modelling and photographs and wouldn't necessarily connect these things. The second was exactly what Sonia asked.

'Somebody? But who? And how could they have heard you if you were locked in your room?'

'You're right, it's a mystery. But I was so distracted and happy, dying to share my joy with somebody, that at the time I didn't even worry about that. My mum had just told me that she thought my father was going to let me make my book. So I was super-excited, and I was singing. And as soon as I realised that was the book that this person was asking about, I replied.'

'You *replied*?' asked Pedro. 'But you didn't even know who'd sent you the message!'

'I know, but at the time I didn't think about it. I just got caught up in the moment. I typed a message in reply, explaining what a model's book is, and pressed send. And hey presto! It disappeared from the screen. And the person obviously received it, because they soon sent me another message, saying "Oh, so you want to be a model!"'

'Then what?'

Colin had been listening quietly all this time, not wishing to interrupt Faye, but when the conversation was running on, he decided to butt in. He greeted Sonia warmly and introduced himself to Pedro and Matt. Then he suggested they move to his office, in the next room, where they could talk privately.

As he asked the secretary to bring some tea and coffee for everyone, he could hear Pedro asking again: 'Then what?'

'Then I replied what you all already know ...' answered Faye, starting to laugh. And the chorus all chimed in with Faye, as she said, 'I-wanna-be-a-model.'

They all laughed. She really did take this teasing from her friends in good humour. Still laughing as they sat around a desk in the office, Faye added, 'What got me curious and made me think was the next message, though. Actually, the two messages that came next. Two questions, which arrived one right after the other – I hadn't even had time to reply to the first one when I got the second.

'If it's a hacker, as you guys say, they must be a very curious hacker. First, he or she asked, "Why not an artist?" And when I was about to reply that I don't really have the talent for the stage, that I'm not very good at singing and don't feel like memorising all those lyrics and stuff – I'd prefer photography studios and the catwalk – I got another message, saying "Model what?".

'I tried to reply, to explain that I want to be a fashion model, to do ads and catalogues, of course – what else could it be? But I couldn't any more. I only answered the first question. After that, it was useless. The message couldn't be sent. Something had gone wrong. I could see that I'd lost contact with the person: it had all disappeared from the phone's memory.'

There was a short, frustrated silence. They were all wondering whether there was a connection between these text messages and the virus or hacker they had come to talk to Colin about. He must think so, anyway, because otherwise he wouldn't have asked Faye to join in the conversation.

The silence didn't last long. Faye soon had a different expression on her face.

'It hadn't disappeared from my own memory, though. I keep thinking about it all the time and asking myself, *What kind of model do I want to be?* I thought it was a breeze, something completely certain, that I've known my whole life, without any doubt. But suddenly I've started to realise I'm not so sure what the answer is any more. A model could be so many different things, things I'd never even thought about before.'

9 – Camille's Friend

Colin began the meeting by explaining why he was interested in talking to the kids. He went back to the first message that had come to his attention, which came mixed up in a legal document, as they all knew. He read that message out loud.

'At the time, I didn't attach much importance to this. I thought it was a piece of homework belonging to one of Andrea's younger sisters.

'But a couple of things did catch my attention. One thing struck me as surprising: this girl must have done her homework really well, because a lot of thorough research had gone into it. She knew stuff that a lot of adults wouldn't have a clue about. For instance, she knew all about how the people of Mesopotamia used reeds to write on clay tablets.'

Here we go again, thought Sonia. *Writing.*

'She knew that women had an important role in that society and were involved in the economic life of the people. You see, the division of labour at the time – you know what I mean? The way the work was divided up between men and women? Anyway, it involved women not only in the production of textiles but also in how businesses were set up and managed.'

Sounded good, Sonia thought, and it did seem to fit in with that message and the list of items for sale and so on.

'But these things changed gradually over the years, and in later societies women's contribution became confined to the domestic arena,' Colin was saying now.

That'd be the home, Sonia thought. Why did he have to call it 'the domestic arena'? Must be a lawyer thing.

'You could say that the Mesopotamian civilisations – the Sumerians, the Akkadians, the Babylonians and the Assyrians – should have been an example to us, but in fact, they have been largely forgotten.'

The young people around the desk looked at each other in dismay. They hadn't bargained on a lecture on … what? Assyrians or something. But there was no stopping Colin now that he'd got into his stride.

'The ancient area of Mesopotamia actually corresponds pretty well exactly to what we call Iraq today,' Colin said, sounding depressingly like a schoolteacher.

They were in for the long haul, they could tell.

'The people of modern Iraq – whom we hear about all the time on the news, people who are victims of the terrible sufferings inflicted by war – are descended from some of the finest civilisations in the history of humankind. Their societies should be role models for us.'

Faye shifted uneasily on her chair. A thought was buzzing in her head like an annoying fly. She was remembering the question that had been asked in the text message on her phone: 'Model what?' her mystery texter had asked.

Now that Colin was using that same word 'model' in a different context, she began to feel uneasy. None of the others noticed.

Colin went on speaking.

'Something else that caught my attention in the message was the way in which the author referred to Hammurabi's legal code.'

Why did all these ancient people have to have such long names? Sonia was thinking.

'This was a pioneering piece of work and a remarkable feat for such an ancient society. We can conclude from the way our mystery messager takes such pride in this achievement that he or she is a person who values justice. More than that: they value a notion of justice that was very innovative at the time and remains fundamental today.'

Colin sounded remarkably like Mr Costa, banging on about all this ancient world stuff and how innovative people had been back then. But there was no way to interrupt him.

'Hammurabi's code says that we can't have double standards in law. In other words, the law cannot be applied on the whim of the king or the leader of the country. The law has to be the same for everyone, and there have to be standard punishments that people know about and that you can expect to have to undergo if you commit certain crimes.'

Yes, well, that made sense. If you could concentrate long enough to understand it.

'Hammurabi adopted the motto "Justice and equity". He was famous for being a wise king and an excellent and even-handed administrator. He was a model sovereign.'

There it was again, that word 'model' which kept buzzing around in Faye's head.

But by this stage, they were all shifting in their chairs, changing their positions, taking sips of water or tea. It was hard to concentrate on what Colin was saying. Do all lawyers have to talk like that and for so *long*?

But Colin didn't seem to notice their discomfort and he carried on.

'Anyway, I didn't pay much heed to the first message. It was only later, when the next message turned up, that I noticed that this message also showed the same interest in justice.

'And I remembered then that Andrea had said something about messages that you had been receiving, some virus maybe. So I examined the messages carefully, and I have to say I didn't think we had a case of a virus here.'

The friends nodded their agreement.

'It just didn't look like a virus to me, and I can imagine you people don't really think it's a virus either.' He paused briefly. 'I cannot shake off the feeling, though,' Colin concluded, 'that this is someone who is in need of help of some sort.'

'Didn't I *say* that?' Matt cut in, very pleased with himself and his powers of deduction. 'It's not a criminal. It's just someone asking for help.'

Maybe they were right, thought Pedro.

The young people went over everything with Colin and showed him the various messages they had kept. They discussed their list of conclusions, and, on Colin's suggestion, they added a new item to it:

• Concerned with justice.

'There's something else that strikes me as strange, though,' said Colin. 'It is very odd that his *modus operandi* is to remain unidentified, hiding behind what seems like a series of pranks and making contact through strange and sudden communications ...'

Nobody knew what *modus operandi* meant. Colin must have noticed their puzzled looks, because he said, 'Sorry, I mean his method of operation.'

They still looked blank.

'His way of doing stuff.' Colin finally got through to them. 'It is odd that he or she chooses to hide behind diverse personalities from entirely different societies and epochs but always under the aegis of the written word, considering it a rare and precious accomplishment.'

Under the aegis of? Whatever that meant! Pedro thought he'd better check if he was following all this.

'Each of the messages comes from a different time and place, is that what you're saying?' he asked. 'And our guy's always all proud because he can read and write. But each time it's different.'

'Exactly!' said Colin. 'And therein lies the mystery.'

'From what my manicurist says, there's no mystery at all,' said Faye. 'Apparently, it's quite common. I had never heard of it myself, but it's probably because we don't know much about these things.'

Her *manicurist*? They all stared at Faye. That was some abrupt change of subject!

Faye explained that she had mentioned the text messages to the manicurist when she went to get her nails done at a beauty parlour on Saturday, and the lady said that one of her neighbours was always receiving messages like that, 'from beyond'.

'Oh, give me a break, Faye,' Sonia snapped. 'Here we are, trying to have a serious discussion, and all you can talk about is this "beyond" nonsense? So now the "beyond" needs computers and mobile phones?'

'No, no, I'm sorry, don't get me wrong. I just used the word "beyond" because it was an easier way to explain the idea – you know, like in the movies. It was the manicurist who said it. Everyone in the salon started talking about this sort of thing then, and they all had things to say.'

'What kind of things?' asked Matt.

'One of the girls said something about past lives. I thought that sounded interesting, and the manicurist thought so too. A lot of people did.'

Sonia threw her eyes up, but Faye took no notice of her friend's scepticism. 'Anyway, this girl said that nowadays there are loads of books about this kind of thing, written by doctors who use hypnosis to treat people. See, they are trying to discover what kind of things happened to their patients in their past lives, because whatever is wrong with them now might have origins in these past experiences.'

'And you *believed* that?' asked Sonia.

'I didn't believe it and I didn't disbelieve it. I've never been hypnotised, I can't remember any past lives, so I don't think I believe it. Actually, I'm sure I don't. But maybe other people do, and I respect that. Why not?'

There was a brief silence.

'Past lives?' said Colin. 'It's an interesting hypothesis. Not that I believe in it myself, but ...'

'But why would these people from the past come to find us in particular, if we're not hypnotised or anything?' argued Pedro.

'Maybe they are us in other times ...' said Faye. 'Or we are them today.'

'Oh, come *on*!' Pedro cut in impatiently. 'Let's stop this nonsense!'

The atmosphere was a bit awkward, filled with an uneasy silence.

'Sorry,' said Faye. 'I just meant that, somehow, we could be some sort of continuation of these people who lived in the past. Like heirs, maybe, or some kind of descendants? Not exactly a new life of these exact people, not really. Oh, I can't explain what I'm thinking, I can only come up with the word continuation. And they are, themselves, the continuation of each other. Those people, I mean. The ones who send us messages.'

This was very mixed up, Sonia thought, but Matt agreed with Faye.

'That's it. That would explain why they come to us when they need help. I mean, we must have something in common with them. Same as we have things in common with each other.'

'Yeah,' said Sonia. 'We do have things in common, of course. We're all friends, classmates, we're the same age –'

'I'm sorry,' interrupted Pedro. 'But not all of us.

The clerk here in Colin's office is not in our class at school, for instance.'

'Still, he might have something else in common with us, but it's just that we don't know what,' Faye said. 'And also, perhaps we have something to do with the person who is sending the messages.'

'That makes sense,' agreed Sonia. 'Perhaps that's why they chose us. But what could it be that we have in common with them?'

'Well, I know she was a model ...' continued Faye.

Everyone laughed.

'A model back in ancient Egypt? Or in an alchemist's tower in the Middle Ages?' joked Pedro. 'And what did she do? She would parade on the catwalk with the latest collections of the tunic designers? Honestly, Faye, sometimes it's like you don't think before opening your mouth ... How did you come up with that?'

'She told me so herself.'

'Who is *she*?'

'Camille's friend,' said Faye.

'*Camille?* Who's Camille?'

'If you would all stop interrupting me, I'll explain.'

Although they weren't feeling very patient, they let Faye talk. She told them that a few days after the series of curious text messages, she got another message, this time on her computer. It was from someone who apologised for having disappeared all of a sudden. (She put that down to a technical problem.) But now here she was, back to introduce herself.

'She said she was a model,' Faye told them, 'and a friend of this Camille person. And, since she had experience in the profession, she wanted to support me. Maybe she believed that, if she could find a way to help me, then I might also find some way to help her, sort of tit-for-tat.

'Being a model was much less work than being an artist, she said, but she had to say it was very tiring work all the same. She said she was sick of it, sitting in the same position for hours, without moving – she must be a photographic model, I suppose – while the artists worked. She would have preferred to follow another path, but she was not as talented as her friend Camille, for instance, who managed to make her own way and create a place for herself in such a masculine world – she did beautiful sculptures.'

Sculptures!

'She went on to say that it was very difficult for women, even if some ladies named Berthe and Mary managed to paint ... she didn't have such talent, or such courage, and that was why she stuck to being a model.'

The others were all gaping at Faye. This didn't make any sense at all.

'But, since she knew how to read and write ...'

They all sat up at that. This was familiar. This

sounded like their Brainy Hacker – and this time, appearing as a female again.

'... she ended up getting another job, in commerce,' Faye was telling them, 'as an assistant in a bookstore, where she could read lots of books and hear bits of conversation from interesting customers. This way, she didn't have to sit completely still, holding the same pose for hours on end, without talking to anybody, so that a whole class could draw and sculpt. It was very tiring.'

'So, she wasn't the kind of model that goes on catwalks showing off outfits or who appears in ads,' Colin concluded. 'She was the kind of model who poses for artists.'

'Of *course*,' said Faye, suddenly getting it. 'That's it. That's the kind of model she was. When one of those first text messages asked me if I wouldn't prefer to be an artist, I thought of musicians and pop stars, that kind of thing. But of course what she meant by "artist" was a painter or a sculptor, the kind of artist she met in *her* work as a model. That makes more sense.'

'What else did you guys talk about?' asked Sonia, wanting to get as much information as possible.

'Not much. She spent the whole time talking about that sculptor, Camille. She seemed really proud of having known this Camille and having met her teacher, Master Rodin.'

'Ah,' said Colin. 'I *get* it. This Camille she was talking about is Camille Claudel.'

Very helpful, Sonia thought sarcastically.

'She was a famous artist in the nineteenth century,' Colin explained, as if he'd overheard Sonia's thoughts.

The others looked at him in amazement. He knew a lot of stuff, and not only about the law.

'There was an exhibition here a couple of years ago,' he explained. 'It showed some of her work. And they also made a movie about her life, I saw part of it on TV. She was the sister of a great French poet and she was the girlfriend of Auguste Rodin, one of the greatest sculptors in history. But she had a tragic life.'

'Yeah, it must be that one,' said Faye. 'The model said Camille ended up crazy, locked up in a mental institution.'

'Well,' Colin said, 'I'm not sure she really was crazy. This movie seemed to suggest it could also be that people wanted to get rid of her because they didn't like her behaviour. She was a very determined woman, and she didn't let obstacles stand in her way.'

Sonia liked the sound of her. Faye too.

'The society of the time did not approve of her,' Colin said, 'but nowadays she is widely recognised as a very talented artist. And she is also highly thought of today because she was such a passionate, rebellious, intense, hard-working woman, way ahead of her time.'

'A model woman ...' said Faye pensively. 'That's exactly what the girl said. At least, that's what arrived in the last text message.'

'There was another one?' Pedro was getting impatient with the way Faye told her story in dribs and drabs.

'Are there any other clues?' asked Matt. 'Did you find out anything else from these messages, Faye?'

'I think I've given you all the facts. She was an artist's model and a friend of this Camille, whom she really admired. But she thought she could be more, she was proud of being able to read and write –'

'Like all the authors of all the messages,' said Sonia.

'And she kept trying to convince me to do the same,' Faye added.

'What do you mean?' asked Pedro. 'Did she try to convince you to be an author of these messages that invade people's computers? Is she looking for accomplices? Did she tell you how she's doing this?'

'No, not that. She said I should dream of something better than being a model. She told me I knew much more than how to read and write, and I could do other things that could be more useful to the world.'

Colin and Pedro didn't notice the brooding expression on Faye's face as she said this. But Matt noticed all right, and he thought she looked even prettier like this, with that dreamy look in her eyes, lost in her thoughts.

'I think there is something we can do,' Colin said, as they went on discussing the whole story. 'Though it's not much. This hacker or joker is managing to communicate with us, right? And he or she has been pretty persistent about it.'

That was true.

'But now we know,' Colin continued, 'from what Faye has told us that it is also possible for us to communicate with the hacker. So this is my idea: I think we should all keep our eyes peeled, and as soon as a new message arrives, we reply immediately.'

'How?' the others wanted to know.

'The same way that Faye did it. A short, immediate response, sent through the same channel as the one used by the hacker. Perhaps one of us will be lucky enough to be able to establish a dialogue in that way. But we need to be on our toes, because we'll probably only get a moment to respond. And whoever makes contact should ask right away what it is that he or she wants and how we can help. That's the only way, I think, by sending a very quick reply, that we will be able to make any progress on this.'

They all thought this was a good idea.

'But with Faye it was different,' said Pedro. 'The person didn't ask for help – did they Faye?'

Faye wasn't so sure about that. 'I don't know, I can't say for sure.' She gave a sigh and then went on. 'She said I had so much opportunity to study and that I shouldn't waste it, but that I should use it to help others.'

'That fits,' said Colin decisively. 'There is always something about the need to help someone. So let's keep our eyes open. As soon as one of us has any news, we should let the others know immediately. I am sure things will become clearer soon. Agreed?'

Everyone agreed.

Pedro had something to add, though.

'I was just thinking. Remember what we were talking about before Faye told us about this friend of Camille's? We were trying to figure out what we could all have in common – us classmates and the clerk from this office – with the mysterious invader. And I have a hunch.'

'What have we got in common, then?' asked Sonia.

'It's that we have all studied, or we are studying – we can all read and write. That's why we can understand the value that our guy puts on literacy.'

'I don't know about that,' said Colin. 'I wouldn't really think that being able to read and write is enough of a link.'

'Yeah, lots of people are literate,' said Sonia, 'especially these days. It's not really a major link.'

'Still, you could be right,' Colin said. 'Our

mysterious hacker is quite possibly communicating with us because he or she thinks we are capable of appreciating words. The messages are not only a cry for help, but you might say they are also a vote of confidence in us. This is one further element for our consideration,' he went on, in his lawyer-like way. 'So let's go our separate ways now and think these things over. Agreed?'

This time, nobody had anything else to add. They all said goodbye and went home.

10 – Rhythm, Poetry and Death

A few days passed before there was any new message from the Brainy Hacker. Little by little, the kids' ordinary day-to-day routine was filled with things that took time or demanded attention: studying for exams, doing homework, playing games, going to a party, to a gig or to the movies. Since the Brainy Hacker hadn't made contact for a while, they gradually put this subject aside. It's not that they had forgotten about it or had become less curious. It was just that other things began to dominate their thoughts and their conversations.

Garibaldi High played a football match one Saturday morning that ended in a draw, despite the total mastery shown by their team. It was bad luck, and it left a bitter taste, because they all knew that their team had played better than the other team.

Afterwards, they all needed to go and have some fun and forget about the match. That's probably why, after the game, Pedro asked Robbie to have lunch at his house. Perhaps later they might play a game with Will on the computer.

'Thanks,' said Robbie. 'That would be cool, but I can't, Pedro. Today is Saturday, remember? I've got the radio show.'

How could he forget? Every Saturday afternoon Robbie became famous. He turned into Robert Freitas and commanded the microphone of the community radio programme, on air for two hours. He talked to everybody, passed complaints along to the authorities, told stories, took phone calls from listeners, interviewed lots of people, played cool songs, presented new bands. He was the closest thing to a celebrity that they had in the group.

'But your programme doesn't start until four,' argued Pedro. 'We've got plenty of time.'

'Yeah, but we're in the middle of the rap contest and I still need to listen to some new stuff that arrived. I'll catch the bus with you, but I'm not getting out at your stop.'

After a pause, Robbie added, 'Actually, the main thing I want is to listen to one particular song again. I've heard it a few times already and I can't seem to reach any conclusion.'

'Is it good? Who wrote it?' Pedro asked as they got on the bus.

'It's a total mystery, Pedro. A really strange rap, from somebody who appeared out of nowhere on the radio's computer without identification or anything and left the recording there. It's quite weird. I can't even tell if it's good or not.'

A quick suspicion crossed Pedro's mind. Could it be? No, it wasn't possible. But ... perhaps.

In any case, he asked, 'How do you mean, it just appeared on the computer?'

'I don't know how it happened. The technician who works on the radio programme thought it might be a virus. Apparently it came in as some kind of encoded message that appeared over another one and came with an attached file. Of course, the tech guy knows better than to open an attachment from a stranger, but it just opened itself, apparently, and the recording was in the attachment.'

'So it appeared out of nowhere, with no explanation?' Pedro was starting to get excited. It *had* to be the same guy.

'Yeah, weird.'

'What about the song, what's it like? Is it good? Is the guy a good singer?'

'As far as rhythm goes,' Robbie said, 'it's quite odd. And his voice is a bit metallic, like it's been distorted, you know? Sort of how robots talk in movies. Or how they distort the voices of testimonies on the news on TV, so that the person won't be recognised later and get into trouble for what they said. Crime witnesses, families of the victim, people that journalists want to protect when they're interviewed. But his rap is not bad.'

Pedro was getting more and more curious. He had to find out more.

'What about the message?' he asked. 'Didn't you say it also came with a weird message that introduced the song?'

'The message was really confusing, all messed up, full of weird little symbols. Like little squares in the places of missing letters, that kind of thing. But I could understand some parts of it. He talked a bit about poetry and asked for help. But it wasn't signed and you couldn't tell who it was from.'

'So how can it be a candidate for the contest?'

'That's the thing. It can't. The rules say that all the contestants have to identify themselves, give their name, phone number, address, so they can be contacted later if they win. This guy can't even be in the running. In any case, I don't think he would win. He wouldn't have much of a chance – there's a lot of really good raps in the competition.'

'But it is a good song?'

'Yes and no. This guy uses strange words. He talks as if he's really old or a foreigner, I don't know. The words exist, but nobody would use them for rapping. It's quite strange. I think that's why I've got the song in my head. It's just different.'

'What is it about?' asked Pedro. 'Can I see it?'

'Death,' answered Robbie.

'Guns? Violence? Gang wars, that sort of thing?'

'No, nothing like that. It's quite different, like I said. I have never heard a song like it before. That's probably why I can't get it off my mind.'

Robbie had a different air about him when he talked about this strange rap. He seemed lost in thought. He paused, scratched his head and then added, 'But it's also about life. I don't know – about the stuff we can use to beat death, about what's left of a person after he's gone.'

'Organ transplants?' asked Pedro, surprised. 'Cryogenic freezing of the body? That kind of thing?'

Robbie laughed. 'No, man, nothing like that. It's not about what's left behind in the hospital or in the cemetery.'

'His *soul*?' suggested Pedro, trying to work it out but feeling a bit embarrassed.

Robbie said, 'No. It's what's left in other people's memories. Sort of like the mark we leave in the world. Everybody leaves some kind of mark, right? Or should leave. Or they're sure they will leave, I don't know. That's why later I kept thinking about this stuff. Hold on, it'll come to me.'

Robbie stopped talking and was clearly trying to remember something. Sure enough, the song came back to him, and soon he was tapping the rhythm on his backpack and singing the words:

I call to you, my brother,
to tell you what's on my mind.
I have come from very far,
I have lived through every kind
of event, through peace and war,
and everything else combined.

But it's like there is a curse and it haunts all of
mankind.
That's when suddenly you find
that your time has come to die.
In a coffin you will lie
and there's nothing left behind.

When he heard the tune, Pedro understood what his friend meant when he said it didn't sound quite like rap. The language was a bit funny for that type of music, and the rhythm was a bit different. Meanwhile, Robbie repeated the chorus, improvising over it.

In a coffin you will lie,
now your time has come to die,
and there's nothing left behind.

It was easy to pick it up. Soon enough, Pedro was singing along. It was fun.

Another boy on the bus, who was in the seat in

front of them, turned towards them and joined in. Robbie repeated the same part again and then continued:

You're thinking you're all that,
you're the man running the show.
You've got fame, lots of girls
and your pockets full of dough,
you are eating caviar
and you live in a chateau.
Everything is going great,
you're just going with the flow.

And then, suddenly, whoa!
No more fun and no more games,
No one remembers your name,
And you're buried down below.

The other kids joined in, singing the new chorus:

And then, suddenly, whoa!
No more fun and no more games,
No one remembers your name,
And you're buried down below.

Then, as more people in the bus started listening to what they were singing, Robbie started the next verse:

Stop that talking, all those words,
all that spoken jamboree.
Singing loud or screaming hard,
words are frail, lost at sea.
If nobody reads it,
then one day it will cease to be.
If it isn't written down,
what's it worth, the poetry?

Then it went back to the first chorus:

That's when suddenly you find
that your time has come to die.
In a coffin you will lie
and there's nothing left behind.

Suddenly, Robbie's voice was recognised. 'Aren't you Robert Freitas, from the radio?'

An old lady wanted to take the opportunity to bring up an issue that he should discuss on the show: the buses were not stopping at the stops for old people.

'They don't stop for kids in school uniforms either,' complained a girl.

'It's the same thing. The drivers can't be bothered stopping for people who don't pay full fare,' said a guy wearing overalls and tapping the beat on a toolbox. 'You should start a campaign on the radio about this kind of behaviour. It's disgraceful.'

110

'Not to mention the lack of respect for people with disabilities,' shouted another voice, coming from the back of the bus.

Everybody had a complaint to make. The music faded. Robbie had to respond: he asked them to call the radio and promised to give a voice to all the complaints.

Pedro was getting impatient. He couldn't wait to talk more about the rap and the message that it had come attached to. He wanted to try and find out whether it could be coming from the Brainy Hacker, now posing as a musician.

But he didn't get a chance to find out any more about it. The bus was almost at his stop. As he stood up, he tried once more to get Robbie to come home to lunch with him.

'I *can't*, I told you,' Robbie replied.

'I need to talk to you about something.'

'So phone me tonight. Or come by the radio station after the show.'

'All right, then. Bye!' Pedro said, as the bus pulled in at his stop.

He was just going to have to wait. In the meantime, the song was stuck in his head. He walked through the door singing:

> *If nobody reads it,*
> *then one day it will cease to be.*

If it isn't written down,
what's it worth, the poetry?

Yes, it could very well be the Brainy Hacker. It was that same story about reading and writing. And a good excuse to call Sonia. Perhaps she'd want to go with him later to meet Robbie at the radio station, so they could talk it over and see if they could find something out? It was always nice to get a chance to see her at the weekend. And with news like that, it was quite natural.

11 – A Frozen Window

'Hello, Pedro? What's up?'

When the phone rang, Sonia was so enthralled by the conversation she was having with Faye that she did something surprising even to herself. Instead of saying 'Hi!' enthusiastically and interrupting everything else to talk to Pedro, as she would usually do, she replied almost automatically, saying, 'I'm sorry, I'm a bit busy. Can I call you later?'

Pedro couldn't exactly put his finger on why, but he felt put out at being treated like that.

'Try not to be too long,' he said. 'It's urgent, Sonia.' And, to pique her curiosity, he added, 'I think it could be important. We might have a really great clue about the Brainy Hacker. But we need to act fast, as time may be running short.'

He was sure that, on hearing this, Sonia would drop everything to talk to him. He was not prepared for the answer he got: 'In that case get over here straight away, because I've also got a great clue and I can't stop now or I'll miss it. Bye.' *Beep. Beep.*

She'd hung up! It couldn't be! But it was. It had happened.

It must have really been something serious, then. He was just going to have to go over to her place. Even though he was starving.

Pedro was permanently starving, actually, but especially when it was past noon, after a hard game of football, with his head spinning at a thousand miles an hour.

He just had to eat something before leaving home. On his way through the kitchen, he grabbed a banana and a slice of bread left over from breakfast and headed towards the door.

'Bye, Mum,' he said as he went. 'I'm off to Sonia's.'

'*Now*, Pedro? We're just about to have lunch!'

'I can't, it's urgent.'

'In that case, take a slice of meat in that bread and make a sandwich that you can eat on the way.'

The meat smelt irresistible, making Pedro's mouth water, so he did as his mother suggested and started to make himself a sandwich.

'Oh, I almost forgot,' said his mother as she sliced the meat. 'That classmate of yours, Faye? She called three times this morning. I told her you were at school, playing football. She said to tell you she was going to Sonia's house.'

Faye? She wanted to talk to *him*?

'Apparently Matt is going too,' his mother went

114

on. 'He also called looking for you and I said you might go to Sonia's house to meet the girls when you arrived home, since Faye was so insistent. But I think he already knew that.'

What was going on? Matt hadn't come to the game because he had the flu. He hadn't been to school the day before either. Perhaps Faye had called him too – and of course, flu or no flu, he could never resist a call from her. They were probably all together at Sonia's house by now. Just like that, on a Saturday morning?

By the time Pedro arrived, the other two had got the gist of Faye's story. She had told it in her usual roundabout way, leaving important information out and putting in things that were totally irrelevant. But by now Sonia and Matt had worked it out, and they were able to sum it up nice and concisely for Pedro, which was just as well, because if he had to hear it at Faye's pace, Pedro really couldn't take it. She was a nice girl, but sometimes she drove him mad, the way she told a story – or rather, the way she didn't tell it.

As soon as Pedro walked in, Matt announced right away: 'The hacker has contacted Faye again, Pedro!'

'How?'

'Well, after what happened last time and all the stuff we talked about, I started thinking a lot about the model-woman thing,' said Faye. 'I decided to do

115

some research online. It was amazing. Who would have thought, I found out that –'

'Faye found out a lot of incredible stuff about what women's lives were like in various places at various times – I'll tell you the details later,' Sonia cut in, kind but firm. 'Anyway, on the website for this university library, there was a form asking her to agree not to use that information for commercial purposes. Then another window popped up asking her to agree not to abandon the written word, not to stop reading books, stuff like that. Right, Faye?'

'I thought it was a bit weird and I didn't quite get it, but I was in a hurry to move on, so I just ticked the box,' Faye explained. 'Then another window appeared asking me to take this commitment to my network of friends. I thought that was even weirder. But once again I agreed and moved ahead. I wanted to search for some stuff and I knew they had a paper about women in Afghanistan under the Taliban regime. Listen, it's amazing how this kind of situation still exists nowadays. After all, it wasn't that long ago. They couldn't study, or work, or go out in the streets – at all, for anything. Not even to buy food. If they didn't have a man in the family, they could starve to death. And since there was a war –'

Sonia interrupted her again. 'Then another message appeared, right, Faye? This time, in big letters.'

'Actually, there were *two* messages on the same window, in two font sizes,' Faye corrected her. 'One of them asked, "IF YOU DON'T READ WHAT'S BEEN WRITTEN, WHAT IS HISTORY WORTH?" The other one, in a larger size, had an exclamation mark at the end: "DO NOT ABANDON YOUR ANCESTORS. READ WHAT THEY HAVE WRITTEN. NO MORE BETRAYAL!" And at the end of it all, almost like a challenge, it said, "SO? ARE YOU GOING TO HELP ME OUT OR NOT?"'

'Just like that?' asked Pedro. 'In those exact words?'

'Yes, I am sure of it, because it was frozen on the screen for a while, it just wouldn't go away, so I had time to memorise it,' said Faye. 'The only way to get rid of that window was to restart the computer. But then it happened all over again. I agreed with everything in the pop-up windows and when I got to that one, the same thing happened. Everything froze. I was stuck on that window. I had to start from scratch yet again.

'But this time, I didn't just tick all the boxes and agree to everything. When I got to that website, the one belonging to the university library, I saw that there was an email address on their contact page.'

'Ah!' said Pedro. 'So?'

'So I sent them a message explaining what had happened.'

'And did they reply?'

'Yeah, they did,' said Faye. 'Only not until the following day. Still, they did get back to me.' She paused for a moment.

'Go on,' said Pedro.

'Well, it wasn't much help, actually. They said it had nothing to do with them.'

'But there was more to it than that,' Matt prompted her. 'Remember what you said about how the library had this big campaign going on about the importance of reading?'

Faye nodded. 'Yes, they told me about that, but they also said that this particular message that I'd got wasn't part of it, as far as they knew.'

'Apparently this reading initiative is pretty big,' Matt added. 'Lots of different institutions are involved in it. They said the message you saw must have been some mistake, maybe brought in through one of the other organisations, but nothing to do with them.'

'Yes, that's right,' said Faye. 'They said they were dedicated to protecting the written word. They said they wanted more people to be involved in the project, that it's the duty of us all, of the whole community. I have their email saved in my inbox. You can read it later if you like, or I could print it out for you.'

Matt said there was no need for her to print out the message, but he might come by her place later to read it and check a few details.

Faye smiled (she smiled!) and said yes, she thought that was a good idea.

Meanwhile, Sonia went back over the rest of the things Faye had told them.

'The thing is, Pedro, the people from the university swore that they were not the ones who wrote that stuff. The two professors who signed the email said they would never use words like that. They were almost offended, saying that this kind of language was not part of their campaign, that they did not use emotional terms such as helping out, abandoning or betrayal. Which kind of makes sense. It's not the way professors speak, is it? So that means –'

Faye cut in. 'They said they must have been hacked by some student trying to be funny or someone trying to derail their project. They apologised for the aggressive tone and promised to take measures to solve the problem.'

'This *has* to have been our hacker again,' said Matt. 'The Brainy Hacker, I mean.'

'*Our* hacker? *Whose* hacker? We've got nothing to do with this stuff,' protested Sonia.

Pedro disagreed. 'I think we have to accept that this is "our" hacker, in a way, Sonia. Because he or she keeps talking to us all the time.'

Sonia didn't argue.

'But, listen,' Pedro went on, 'I think it might be a good idea to contact the university again and tell them the whole story. I mean, look, they have a lot of resources. They would be in a much better position to tackle this whole business than we could possibly be. They have much better security systems, for a start.'

'Yeah, could be,' said Sonia. 'But look, on the other hand, they jumped to the conclusion that it was probably one of their students who was to blame for this.'

'So?' said Pedro.

'Well, I think that means they are suspicious of young people. So they could easily start thinking it's our fault. I think we should steer clear of these people, or we might end up in trouble.'

'But they can investigate this stuff much better than we can,' argued Pedro. 'They can dig deeper.'

The others weren't sure. They thought about it for a while.

Then Faye spoke up. 'You have a point, Pedro, when you say that talking to the university people might be a good thing. They're a large institution, as you say, and they must have a legal department as well as a really big IT department, all sorts of stuff. They really have a much better chance of solving this mystery than we have.'

Pedro smiled. At last, someone recognised how right he was.

'But ...' Faye went on, 'Sonia has a point too. The

thing is, we don't want people to start suspecting that we are responsible for this whole thing.'

'So what do you suggest, Faye?' asked Matt eagerly.

'Well, I think the best thing would be to talk to Colin again. He's a lawyer, remember, and we promised him we'd get back to him if there were any more developments.'

So they had.

'So I think the best thing is to let Colin deal with it for us. Then we won't have anything to worry about – that's what the law is for, isn't it? To defend the citizens and make sure that everybody in society is respected. I mean, look, suppose you have a case of domestic violence, for example. If all you could depend on was some random police officer who got called in to the case, the woman might end up completely defenceless. If there were no ...'

Her friends were speechless. This really didn't seem like the Faye they had known for all these years, launching into a speech like that on the value of the law and the importance of justice. She usually came across as so ditzy. And yet, they all knew in their hearts that there was more to Faye than she let on. Something had given her the courage to speak up, clearly and fluently and confidently.

Matt, of course, was completely enthralled. Faye was more beautiful than ever when she was like this, her eyes sparkling with the excitement of what she was saying,

Sonia was about to make a joke about Faye's oratorical skills, when Pedro cut in quickly to bring them back to the subject.

'Great idea, Faye! I think we can all agree on this. We should definitely talk to Colin. Right, everyone?'

The others all nodded.

'But we can't really get in touch with him until Monday, so just for now, let's see if we can think our way through this a bit more.'

They all looked at him expectantly.

'As I see it,' Pedro continued, 'our hacker has made an important move here. He's made a much more daring approach, using a much bigger, more powerful website, with a higher risk of leaving a trail. He's taking a bigger risk to get close to us.'

Well, that seemed to make sense. But did it get them anywhere?

'And by the way,' Pedro went on, 'I have something else to tell you. Robbie told me something earlier today that also suggests that the Brainy Hacker is making new moves. But one thing at a time. Remind me to tell you later, when we've finished discussing this thing of Faye's.'

He turned to Matt then and asked, 'What do you think, Matt?'

'I agree. I mean, I agree with what you said just

now and also with Faye's idea about talking to Colin when we get a chance. But I also want to say that I think this whole story confirms what I've been saying for a while: this guy is somebody who's in trouble and wants us to help him.'

'That's right!' said Sonia. 'You have been saying that all along, Matt, and you are right. But now we know what he wants.'

Everyone turned to listen to Sonia. She was saying what they had all known all along, in a way, but hadn't quite put into words.

'What he's been begging us to do all the time is not to stop reading.'

That was true, but it seemed such a weird request. 'But *why*?'

Faye's question was left unanswered, because just at that moment, Sonia's mother came to offer them some lunch.

'I didn't know you were all coming – Sonia never said. But I have got together a nice lunch of black beans and rice, and manioc flour with eggs. A delicious *feijoada* for everybody. And some salad.'

Apart from Faye, who was always keen to eat healthily, nobody was too interested in the salad part. But they were very hungry. So the discussion was immediately interrupted and they all went to lunch.

12 – Gregorio Alvarenga's Dedication

It wasn't until they were eating ice cream for dessert that Sonia remembered to ask Pedro. 'Didn't you say you had something new to tell us? Something about Robbie? What is it?'

Pedro swallowed his last spoonful, took a sip of water and then told them about the conversation he had had with Robbie on the bus. He even sang the bits he could recall from the mysterious rap song Robbie had received from some anonymous contestant.

'So you think the Brainy Hacker is playing the part of a rapper now?' asked Sonia sceptically.

'I think it has to be him again,' said Matt. 'There's something familiar about this – it's the same method of communication, the way all those other messages popped up unexpectedly on computers.'

'Or on a mobile phone,' added Faye.

'Yes, but that's much the same thing. A mobile and a computer both use chips. They are both communications devices, and they are both capable of being intercepted in this way.'

'Yeah,' said Sonia. 'I suppose.'

'I think this has to be our man again,' said Matt. 'We shouldn't ignore any leads at this point. Pedro's right. This is really urgent.'

Sonia was starting to feel drowsy after the good lunch they'd just had. 'Urgent?' she asked lazily. 'Why?'

'Because today is Saturday!' said Pedro and Matt in unison.

The girls burst out laughing, remembering a poem they had all learnt at school, where 'Because today is Saturday' was the refrain.

Pedro explained what he meant. 'I'm not sure if you are all fans of Robbie's Saturday radio show? It's really good, actually, and a lot of people listen to it. Anyway, he spends all Saturday afternoon at the radio station, doing the show live. I told him I'd meet him there after the programme to talk some more about this thing that's happened. But now it occurs to me, what if our hacker friend tries to make contact again? And what if it happens today? If it does, I want to be there. Remember how Colin said we should try to respond to any of these messages if we get a chance?'

'So now you can see what he means by saying it's urgent,' Matt said.

'It's dead urgent,' said Pedro. 'In fact, I think I'd better not wait till the end of the programme. I'm heading over there now, before it starts, to make sure I'm there if anything happens.'

'Great idea!' said Matt. 'We'll all go!'

A few minutes later, all four of them were on a bus on the way to the radio station. They arrived just a little after the programme had started.

As they went past reception, they could hear Robbie's voice coming through the speakers. He had just finished presenting the first item, an interview with a community leader about a group of sewing-machine operators who had formed a cooperative to participate in a fashion event. After a short jingle, Robbie announced, 'Now, don't change the station, it's time for a dedication!'

That was how he always announced the part of the programme in which people phoned in to dedicate a song to someone. After the introductory sentence, Robbie played the little jingle again and then said, loud and clear: 'And now, Gregorio Alvarenga dedicates this song to Pedro, Sonia, Faye, Matthew and William.'

The four friends exchanged surprised glances. 'That's us!'

It was startling to hear their names being announced in Robbie's voice – Robert Freitas, the famous broadcaster – and to hear that someone was dedicating a song to them on the radio, just at the very moment they were all – except for Will –

walking into the building. As the first chords of the song started playing, it dawned on them that not only was this a coincidence, it was also a mystery.

'Who?'

'I don't know!'

'Do you know anyone named Gregorio Alvarenga?'

'Not me!'

They were still heading for the studio. Pedro knew his way around the radio station, and the staff knew him too. He and Matt had often been there to meet Robbie, so nobody bothered them. As they walked, this was the song that was playing: 'I was born about ten thousand years ago ...'

'Oh, no!' cried Matt, the first to realise what was going on. 'It's our hacker. The guy is sending us a musical message! He's finally decided to tell us who he is.'

'Gregorio Alvarenga? Gregorio Alvarenga?' repeated Pedro. 'Where does that name come from? Reminds me of something. A poet, maybe?'

'But this is a real song, it exists,' said Sonia. 'I've heard it. My dad has that album.'

As they arrived at the studio door, they all stopped. A red light was turned on over the door.

'We can't go in,' said Matt. 'The light's on. He's on air. We'll have to wait outside.'

That was disappointing. They were going to have to hang around, either in the corridor or in a little room next door, where there were a few chairs. They could sit and listen to the rest of the programme while they waited to talk to Robbie. But Pedro didn't want to sit around waiting.

'No,' he said firmly. 'I'm going in.'

'What about the red light?' said Matt. 'You can't go in. You'll be in the way.'

'He's on air, but he's not talking right now. It's just music. I've seen a technician going in and out more than once. I won't disturb anyone. Robbie is in the isolation booth. I'm going in. If anyone else wants to come, do it now.'

Faye hardly had time to wonder what an isolation booth could mean. She pictured something like a solitary confinement cell in a jail. It didn't seem very likely that Robbie would be stuck in one of those. Pedro put his finger to his lips for silence, and already he was opening the heavy door. Sonia stuck close to him and slipped in with him. Matt was following the other two, and Faye, who didn't want to be left alone outside, grabbed Matt's hand.

This almost ruined everything. Matt got such a shock at the touch of her hand that he stood paralysed for a second, unable to move forward. Through the half-open door, Faye could see Pedro and Sonia already inside, and beside them was a console covered in buttons and switches. The console was being operated by a technician, who was facing a glass wall that separated him from a cubicle. That must be what they called the isolation booth, Faye figured, because on the other side of the glass wall Robbie was sitting at a desk, wearing headphones. In front of him was a microphone and a lot of scattered sheets of paper.

The technician turned to them and immediately started telling them off.

'Hey! You can't come in here! Close that door!'

From the other side of his glass wall, Robbie had seen them and waved hello. Then he closed his fist and gave a thumbs-up, indicating to the technician that it was alright, they could stay. The guy went on grumbling, complaining, making hand signals and pointing at the door.

All this time, Matt didn't budge. He just stood there, holding Faye's hand and feeling his heart going *thump-thump-thump*, beating louder than the sound of the programme that was on air. Surely the whole neighbourhood could hear it, banging away at who-knew-what decibel level.

Faye put her mouth close to his ear and whispered, 'Go on! Get inside!'

Matt stumbled in, feeling dizzy, not letting go of her hand. If it were up to him, he would keep hold of this little hand for ever. Faye, using her left hand to push back the heavy door they had entered, seemed to have forgotten that the fingers of her right hand were still wrapped around his.

Meanwhile the technician was giving a list of instructions.

'OK, watch it now. Keep quiet. He's going on air.'

He pressed a little button and talked into a microphone so Robbie could hear him inside his booth.

'Ten seconds.'

Robbie cleared his throat, while the technician turned a huge button on the console and slowly turned down the volume of the music, bringing the song to an end.

Then Robbie announced, 'Gregorio Alvarenga has just dedicated "I Was Born About Ten Thousand Years Ago" to his friends. And here he is, to talk to us briefly ...

'He's *here*?'

Sonia was alarmed. She expected the guy would just walk right into the studio, in the flesh. She wasn't used to listening to Robbie's show and didn't know he often chatted on the phone with a person who was dedicating a song.

'Good afternoon, Gregorio. How are you?'

The answer was in a metallic voice, coming from one of the big speakers.

'Never been better, Robert.'

It was in sharp contrast to Robbie's voice, which

was full, warm and articulate, like a professional broadcaster.

'Very good, Gregorio. And where are you from? Where do you live?'

'Oh, one day here, one day there ...' answered the voice. 'I am of no fixed abode.'

While the friends listened to this in surprise, Pedro picked up a pen from the table and started writing something on a sheet of paper in big bold letters, easy to read from the other side of the glass.

The conversation continued: 'Yet another listener with housing problems, my friends ... And what do you do for a living?'

'I've been doing a bit of everything throughout these lives ...' was the answer.

These lives? Sonia and Faye exchanged glances. Pedro had just finished writing and raised the sheet of paper to show Robbie. Matt was still hypnotised by Faye's hand in his own, as if he were frozen. Or as if they were not even there.

From the other side of the glass, the broadcaster Robert Freitas read Pedro's message: 'ASK IF THAT'S REALLY HIS NAME.'

Robbie was well used to improvising. Now he said, 'We have here with us our listener of the day, Gregorio ... I'm sorry, Gregorio. Could you please repeat your name for us?'

'Gregorio ... de ... Gonzaga,' said the voice, hesitant.

'Gonzaga? Or was it Alvarenga?' Robbie suggested, checking one of the sheets of paper in front of him. This time the answer came without any hesitation:

'Gonzaga or Alvarenga. It's all the same. Like Gregorio, it doesn't matter. They are all poets. And brave. Masters of the written word.'

Pedro scribbled furiously on another sheet of paper, while Robbie continued the interview.

'Well, well, the names of many famous Brazilian poets rolled into one! So, your parents were very fond of poetry and your name is Gregorio de Gonzaga Alvarenga, a tribute to many poets?'

Now he could see the other sheet of paper that Pedro was holding up: 'SAY THAT WE'RE HERE.'

Meanwhile, the metallic voice was replying, 'The name does not matter. A name ... What's in a name? I could be named after a whole team, because I am many.'

On the other side of the glass wall, the technician laughed out loud and commented, 'This guy's completely insane! Must be calling from a mental institution! I'd like to see how Robert gets out of this one ...'

But Robbie seemed pretty comfortable. He continued to chat with the person with the metallic voice.

'My dear Gregorio Alvarenga, I think I have a surprise for you. Your friends to whom you have just dedicated that song, at least some of them, are here with us in the studio. I would love to say that our producers did a whole lot of teamwork to locate them, but I'd rather tell the truth. It's just an amazing coincidence, because they are my friends too and have just dropped by to see me.'

'I know ...' answered Gregorio – or whoever was the owner of that voice, with his whole array of names.

What did he know? That they were there? Or that they were friends with the broadcaster? But Robbie didn't even seem to hear those two short words, because he went on talking. 'If you like, you can say a few words. To all of our listeners, of course. But especially to them, since they're almost all here.'

'Almost all? Why? Who is missing? Is Faye there?'

As Robbie was explaining that the only one missing was William, something surprising happened. When he heard Faye's name pronounced by that metallic voice, Matt suddenly snapped out of the paralysed state he had been in. He let go of Faye's hand, stepped up to the console and pressed a little button – the one that had been used a moment ago to activate the microphone in the outer room and allow communication with the booth, when the producer had told Robbie he would be on air in ten seconds.

Everyone heard Matt's voice sounding over the conversation, transmitted live to the whole community of listeners. 'What's the deal, man?' he said to this Gregorio person. 'Why are you so interested? And what do you want with Faye?'

'Calm down, my boy, I just asked because I've spoken to her before,' answered Gregorio God-knows-what, in his metallic, computer-distorted voice.

'Well, now you can talk to all of us,' replied Matt, with his finger still on the button.

From the other side of the glass, Robert Freitas tried to take control of the situation. In the outer room, the technician took Matt's hand off the control, while Robbie addressed the listeners.

'My friends, you have just heard one of the people to whom this afternoon's song has been dedicated. Matt, who is on a visit to our studio, has been asking a few questions of Gregorio Alvarenga. This is Vila Teodora Community Radio, with the Robert Freitas show, always on the air to make friends and give everyone a voice. So, Mr Gregorio Alvarenga, what have you got to say to us?'

'Well, as a representative of the poets, all I have to say is that the verses we write are waiting for readers to come and find our poems, and find in them the emotions and thoughts that have travelled over distances and have conquered time.'

Thinking that he really needed to put an end to this crazy conversation and carry on with his show, Robbie prepared to say goodbye before playing another jingle and passing on to another segment of the programme.

'Very well, this has been Gregorio Alvarenga, today's participant listener. Thank you so much for your words, on behalf of all our listeners.'

On the other side of the glass, the technician relaxed, glad that the tension created by all these improvisations and interruptions had lifted. He was just about to play the jingle, as soon as Robbie gave him the signal, but then Matt, seeing that the technician had let his guard down, pressed the little button again. Only this time he had had time to think and put his ideas in order, so he was able to say, calmly and objectively: 'This is Matt here again. I'm sorry, Gregorio, but before you leave, could you please quickly tell us whether you need any assistance? And what can we do to help you?'

Robbie tried to get control of the situation again. 'Very briefly, please,' he added, 'as we're running out of time.'

'Yes,' said Gregorio, 'I do need help, and lots of it. Actually, I must confess that is the reason I am here. I am making use of this radio show to ask for help. For a long time now, I have noticed how Robert Freitas does such a great job on this show, helping people. So you're quite right, I really do need help.'

This comment disarmed Robbie. There was still plenty of time – the programme still had nearly two hours to run – and at this stage, he really couldn't just cut off this Gregorio de Gonzaga or Alvarenga or whatever his name was and take him off the air. There was nothing for it but to let him continue.

'In that case,' said Robbie, 'please explain to us your problem. But please, try to be concise.'

'Can I tell you my story? It's necessary for you to understand.'

'Briefly, please, keep it short.'

'Well, I think we can say, to put it briefly, that I worked for a while in a laboratory, and there was a bit of an accident. I was splashed by one of the products that my master was using, and I have had to live with the consequences. For ever.'

Ah, a work-related injury. Something concrete, at last. Robbie was used to hearing stories like this. He was more comfortable with this. He knew what kind of things he should say in this situation. He could carry on with the programme.

'We've had cases like this on the show before. We have a lawyer, in fact, who can give you some guidance. What our friend needs to do is write us a letter, explaining the whole thing in detail, what happened, the name of the company, whether there were any witnesses and so on. All the details you have. It would be good, too, if you could let us have some proof, maybe a medical report or an eyewitness account, a police report, even, if you happened to report the incident to the police at the time. We will study your situation carefully and forward your request for compensation.'

While Robbie was saying all this on the radio, his friends in the outer room of the studio were discussing the whole thing. Of course they knew what this was about. It was that incident with the wizard, the story the Brainy Hacker had told through Will's computer game. Some of the Elixir of Youth had dropped on him and he had become like a zombie, floating around throughout the centuries. And now here was this guy confirming the story.

'No, no,' Gregorio was saying. 'I'm not looking for compensation. I just want to rest.'

'And how can we help?' asked Robbie. 'Would you like to be sent to some kind of clinic maybe, for a bit of R and R?'

They all listened carefully. On both sides of the glass. And the whole radio audience must have been listening too.

'That's why I took part in the rap contest,' said Gregorio. 'With my song on this subject.'

Robbie immediately recognised the rap he was referring to, and he sang one of the verses:

If nobody reads it,
then one day it will cease to be.
If it isn't written down,
what's it worth, the poetry?

Robbie was back in charge of the show now.

'So it was you who wrote that song? In that case, we're talking to an old friend of this show. But I didn't know it was you, because I didn't recognise the name you used today when you dedicated the song.'

'That's because I used a different name this time,' said the metallic voice. 'But the message I am trying to get across is that poetry is eternal. Stories too. Literature is eternal. That's what endures. Not us. People keep changing, some die, others are born. But what is written down is what endures. The written word crosses time and space; it communicates with those who are far away. It doesn't matter whether it's a letter or an email, a book or a parchment. Words are the mark we leave on the world.'

There! thought Robbie. There was no doubt about it, the guy was delirious. He was going to have to cut this speech short somehow.

'Our friend is right,' he announced. 'Thank you for reminding us. But now our time is up and we have to say goodbye.'

'Just one last thing,' insisted the metallic voice. 'The human spirit lives forever in books –'

'All right, thank you.'

'... and when the books are read,' continued the voice, not stopping even to take a breath, not giving Robbie a chance to cut him off (because you really can't hang up halfway through a sentence), 'the human spirit stays alive for ever, it doesn't die, and then I can rest because everything that humanity has ever done will continue here, present, helping everyone who is born anywhere, but if reading disappears, I go back to my damnation, my enchantment, my curse, condemned to wander forever, it's dangerous, it's a huge risk, it's –'

Robbie couldn't take any more. The programme was already a mess. Things couldn't go on like that. He signalled to the technician, gesturing counter-clockwise with his hands.

The technician knew what he meant and started slowly turning a big button on the console, while with his other hand he slowly turned a different button in the opposite direction. The sound of the metallic voice slowly faded, as the sound of the jingle got louder. So ended the conversation with Gregorio de Gonzaga, or Alvarenga, or whoever he was. The Brainy Hacker. The Poetic Hacker, maybe they should call him now. The wizard's assistant, who travelled through time defending the written word and who had pestered the friends for so long.

13 – Like a Movie

You know how sometimes you get information at the end of a movie or a TV programme, just a few sentences about what happened to the characters after the story ends?

Johnny is in prison.

Jack and Jill got married and moved to the Bahamas.

Mr So-and-so became president of the company.

Rosie and Roger had triplets and opened a stall selling watermelons in a farmer's market in Cornwall.

That kind of thing.

I thought I might end this book that way too – but not just yet. I have a bit more to tell you first, about what happened when Robbie's radio show ended.

The kids stayed for a while around the radio station, hanging out, waiting for Robbie to come off air.

The mysterious Gregorio Alvarenga didn't show up again. Not there and not anywhere else. Not under this name or any other. Not on mobile phones, computer games or email attachments. The Brainy

Hacker just disappeared as suddenly as he had come. Except for one last message that Robbie got as he was getting ready to leave the studio that Saturday.

The four friends who'd been at the radio station phoned Will, and he came over to meet them. Robbie soon joined the others after the show, and they all went to get a bite to eat. They had a lot to talk about.

The first thing was this one last email that had arrived on the station's computer after the end of Robbie's show. It was addressed to the famous broadcaster Robert Freitas 'and today's guests'.

There was no readable identification in the header, just some numbers and letters mixed randomly, as if they were encrypted. The subject line read 'Message for you'. After that it was all clear. You could read the whole message and understand everything. No squiggly characters, no mysteries:

My friends,

It's quite possible that this greeting, on the very day that we met, will also be a goodbye. I know you will help me, now that you've understood the trouble that has been afflicting me for so long.

You will surely come to my rescue, as you have understood that I am a spirit wandering throughout eternity. With this help you will give me, it's possible that we will no longer need to have this kind of direct contact in the future.

Perhaps I will miss you. I have grown to appreciate and care for each of you. Yes, I will miss you, I admit it. But I will no longer suffer.

Either way, we can always meet again, in the best possible way: on the pages of the books you read, with the joy and the awe of discoveries. In other words, in the situation for which words and the way to transmit them has been created so that they can persist. The written language and its reading. This is what allows human beings to travel through time and conquer death.

There he goes again, the friends were all thinking privately. All this waffle about reading. But still they read on, kind of interested at the same time.

Back in Ancient Greece, Hippocrates wrote: 'Life is short, art is long'. People still quote this saying today.

I think it is part of human nature to be conscious that everything is fleeting and one day we shall die. Other animals do not share this awareness. But along with this knowledge of how things pass comes the human desire to conquer death. That is also part of the human condition.

Yes, they'd got that part. Ages ago.

In the Middle Ages, alchemists like my master searched for an elixir that would allow them to survive throughout the centuries, individually, in the flesh. They did not realise that that is not the way to conquer time. We can only achieve this collectively, as a species, through the history of all people, by passing things along.

The friends looked at one another. But still they read on. They'd got used to their Brainy Hacker's rambling ways and strange use of language.

For this to work, we need memories, transmitted from one generation to the next, and the way we preserve those memories is through the written word.

They sighed. Same old, same old.

Because those droplets fell on me all those centuries ago in the alchemist's laboratory, a small part of my spirit has been unable to die. My individual consciousness has been aware of all kinds of writings and memories throughout time. And this has meant that I have never been able to rest. No individual can stand this. We all need the balance between memory and oblivion. Forgetting is a necessary blessing. Not only is life more brief than art: that is the way it is supposed to be.

It is bad enough that I am condemned to half-live for ever, but when I started to feel worried recently that people might be forgetting how important the written word is, that they are in danger of abandoning literature in favour of the image – well, that made me more restless than ever. I began to think that nature itself and the future of this planet were under threat from the rampant advancement of new technologies invented by men. I became truly worried about humankind's destructive capabilities.

That is why I felt I had to reach out to you and try to convince you of the value of reading. I am now more at ease. I managed to make contact with you and I am certain that you have understood me. So now I can rest.

I wish you a long and happy life, immersed in still longer art.

Many thanks,

Best regards from

Gregorio Alvarenga Gonzaga Dias Bilac Bandeira Drummond de Castro Alves …

The list faded away, mixing names of many famous poets, until it finally became illegible.

The friends read the message, curious and touched. There was silence for a few moments, and then they all suddenly started talking.

'That's a bit clearer …'

'They're all poets, those names.'

'Yeah ...'

'We can understand what the guy wanted. Sort of.'

'Maybe he's not all that crazy ...'

They went on talking then, about everything that had happened over the time in which the Brainy Hacker had visited them. Everything that has been told here and that you already know. They went over it all again, as if they were afraid they might forget.

The story was, of course, incredible. At the same time, they'd had the experience. They'd read the messages. The best they could do was *pretend* it was all true, even if they knew it couldn't be. And after all, that's how all stories work, really, whether it's in books, movies or on TV. We all know it's not real, but we go along with it, and that allows us to be entertained, touched, excited, to become thoughtful and to learn stuff.

So the friends decided to pretend to believe the whole daft story about how, a long time ago, some drops of liquid that were being tested as a component of the Elixir of Youth fell on an alchemist's assistant. Part of this person, touched by that liquid, ended up existing forever. Not in body, but in spirit. Precisely the part that can live in everything that humankind writes, and that allows humans to conquer distance and time and allows them to communicate with future generations.

And then somehow he'd got hold of the idea that writing and literature were under some kind of threat, and he mounted a very weird kind of one-man reading-promotion programme, aimed at this particular group of friends.

Why them? Nobody knows. Least of all them, but he seems to feel now that he has gotten his point across.

This is all, of course, nonsense in the opinion of our friends. They didn't really get the connection he had made between his own situation and the threat he thought the written word was facing. But he did genuinely seem to fear that if nobody read any more, he would end up lost, floating and fluttering forever, like waves lost in space, formed by the reverberation of words that had been spoken and written in the past and that nobody would receive in the future.

Sonia, Pedro, Matt, Faye, Will and Robbie didn't think that reading and writing were coming to an end. Still, just to be on the safe side, and because they felt a kind of loyalty to the weird Brainy Hacker, they thought they would give a little hand.

Robbie decided to include a segment on book discussions in his radio show – and it was really successful. Listeners would call in to suggest books for people to read, and they would have debates about what they read.

Also, the friends got in touch with the university library that was running the reading campaign –

the one Faye came across when she was doing her research. And they all participated in that campaign to promote reading. Garibaldi already had a library, so they campaigned for other schools in their area to create cool spaces for people to read in. At their own school, they held a fair to collect funds to buy more books and to hire a full-time professional librarian. They suggested putting a bookcase in the staffroom so that the teachers could have books to read. Each teacher brought books and left them there for whoever wanted to borrow them. They liked the idea of students encouraging teachers to read!

The things the kids did must have helped a lot, because Gregorio Alvarenga never showed up again. They reckoned he must be resting, like he wanted to.

Well, now all we're missing is that end-of-movie stuff. Some of these details you've probably guessed already.

Pedro and Sonia are going out.

So are Matt and Faye.

Will created a new game, full of book tips. He sold the project to a gaming company in São Paulo and made a lot of money.

Robbie was invited to produce a teen-time segment on a cable TV channel. He's an even bigger celebrity now.

Andrea graduated and got married to Colin.

Carol is still exactly the same, only older. But she

still loves butting in where she isn't invited. Luckily, she now has her own set of friends and spends the day on the phone, enjoying her own conversations, so she doesn't need to snoop so much on other people's.

Everything as expected, no surprises. Except for Faye.

Faye gave up on being a model. Now she wants to be a role model. She still doesn't know whether she's going to study journalism or law, she's just sure that she wants to help defend women who are trafficked or abused or have their human rights disrespected. She's really hopeful that things will improve and wants to work professionally on behalf of women. At least, that's what she says. And writes. Faye has a blog about this stuff. But she also writes about other things and reads all the time. If it's up to her, Gregorio (de Matos), (Tomás Antônio) Gonzaga, Alvarenga (Peixoto) and all the other poets can rest in peace.

I'd better stop now, because otherwise this could go on for ever. That's how reading works. You start by discovering one thing, then one book or story leads to another and the subject never ends. There's always something new, so much variety. Just like life.

But this book must end. So I will drop a full stop here … unless you would like to carry it on yourself. Be my guest.

Think About It

1 – Project Mystery

Right, so you've read the first chapter and it's all a bit mysterious. But before we think about that, let's get the characters straight in our heads.

1. *What's the history teacher's name?*
2. *Who was the leader of the project team?*
3. *Whose house did the team meet in to do the project?*
4. *Which of the characters likes to think about food?*
5. *Who is interested in fashion and make-up?*

The project the kids did was about ancient Egypt and the pharaohs. Were you able to follow the stuff that Mr Costa read out? See what you can remember:

1. *Which pharaoh died very young and had a fabulous tomb full of gold and jewels?*
2. *Which pharaoh changed the religion of Egypt?*
3. *What was the name of the sun-god that this pharaoh worshipped?*
4. *What was the name of the wife of this pharaoh? And what was she most famous for?*

It might be fun to choose one of the four figures mentioned in the project (one of the two pharaohs, or the wife, or the sun-god) and look up a bit more about them on the internet or in a book about ancient Egypt.

2 – Nefertiti

Well! It's all very odd, and the message from Nefertiti is quite hard to follow, isn't it? That's probably because she isn't writing in her own language, and because she comes from thousands of years ago. You don't need to try to work out what every sentence means; it's enough to just get the drift.

We don't know which website Sonia went to, but it would probably have been in Portuguese. You could take a look at this one, to get an idea of the kind of thing she saw:

www.ancientegypt.co.uk

You could probably find more sites like this, if you are interested in hieroglyphics.

One of the main things Nefertiti says in her weird message is that she was one of very few girls who learned to read and write in her time. If you are a girl, do you think it would have been good to live in a time when girls didn't learn to read? You probably wouldn't have had to go to school, of course. If you are a boy, you might think it would be fine if girls didn't learn to read and write. There wouldn't be any of them at school, for a start. But would it be fair?

Just think of all the things you like to do that you couldn't do if you weren't able to read and write. You could make a list if you like (which of course you wouldn't be able to do if you couldn't write!).

3 – The Brainy Joker Strikes Again

Weirder and weirder ...

First, let's make sure we've got the characters right. Draw lines to link the characters to the sentences that describe them. (Answers at the back of the book.)

Andrea Is cross with her older sister for using her computer
     Has a colleague called Colin
     Is electric in the mornings, once she gets going

Carol   Is an intern in a law firm
     Is a lawyer
     Drives a car

Colin   Understands Sonia's morning grumpiness
     Is the youngest in the family

Now, take a look at the weird list. Have you any idea what a comb for wool is? Can you find out?

Do you think the longer message is from the same person as before? If you think it is from Nefertiti again, what makes you think that? If you think it is from someone else this time, what makes you think that?

It might be a good idea to find out who Hammurabi was. Why do you think the person sending the message mentions Hammurabi?

4 - A Clue - Maybe

Do you think Pedro could be right about Mr Costa playing tricks on them? If so, why? If not, why not?

Do you think Pedro is right about Marco Polo? (You might have to look up Marco Polo to find out.)

What clues do Sonia and Pedro have about the Brainy Joker? Make a list of all the things they know about the person who has been sending the messages. Does this give you any clues as to who it might be?

5 – Double Trouble

So, the Brainy Hacker has struck for a second time in Andrea's office, this time interfering with an important deed. It's all very strange.

What do you think of Andrea? Can you think of a word that sums her up?

Why do you think Faye might want to talk to Andrea? What could it be about?

6 – A Matter of Strategy

So now the messages are coming from someone with a Portuguese-sounding name. And then there was also that brief message on the computer screen from the wizard's assistant. We've come a long way from Nefertiti in ancient Egypt. Have you any idea what is going on?

Will gives Sonia a bit of a lecture about the importance of alchemy in the Middle Ages. Can you remember the three things he said the alchemists were trying to discover? It might be a good idea to look up alchemy and see if you can find out anything else that might make it all a bit clearer.

Do you believe the story about the drop of liquid falling on the wizard's assistant that seemed to give him some sort of eternal life?
Do you think the boys believe it?
What about Sonia?

The Brainy Hacker mentions 'new technologies' and

sends his messages through computers. What other ways do you think this person might contact Sonia and her friends?

7 – Message in a Bottle

This latest message is stranger still, isn't it? Why do you think the kids are saying the hacker is now claiming to be a priest?

Can you find out anything about Jesuit missions to South America? Does that help to throw any light on what is going on?

Do you agree with Matt when he says he thinks the person is looking for help?

What do you think about Pedro's idea that the person might be a criminal? Do you think that's very likely, or is he being a bit paranoid?

What would you do if you were one of them? Would you go on trying to work it all out, or would you go and talk to someone?

Do you think Colin is a good choice of person to talk to?

8 – Model What?

We haven't really met Faye much in the story so far. What is your impression of her?

Matt is very concerned that Faye was approached by a stranger in the street. Do you think he is right to be worried about this?

Faye has always wanted to be a model, but now she is beginning to question what the word 'model' actually means. What do you think is going on in her head? Can you think of different kinds of model, apart from a fashion model?

9 – Camille's Friend

We've been hearing about Colin all along, but this is our first time to really hear him talking. What kind of person do you think he is?

Colin wants the kids to add 'Concerned with justice' to their list of things about the mystery sender of the messages. Do you think that this really is a point about the messenger? Or are there other things about him or her that you think are more important?

What do you make of Faye's story about the manicurist and the other people she met at the beauty parlour? Sonia and Pedro are not very impressed with that story. What do you think about it?

Colin tells them about Camille Claudel, who was a very famous sculptor at a time when women were not really supposed to be artists. You could look her up and see if what Colin has to say is right.

Did you notice that two other first names of female artists are also mentioned – Berthe and Mary. These are probably Berthe Morissot and Mary Cassatt, who were both painters at around the same time as Camille Claudel was doing her sculptures. You could research these artists to see what interesting things you can find out about them.

Now that you know the characters in the story a lot better, which one do you like best?

10 - **Rhythm, Poetry and Death**

Do you think Pedro is right, that the rap song is also a kind of message from the Brainy Hacker?

What do you think of the rap? Do you agree with Robbie that it sounds a bit strange? What's strange about it?

From the conversation on the bus, what kind of radio show do you think Robbie hosts?

_11_ - **A Frozen Window**

The hacker has changed his or her tactics over the last little while. Instead of sending long messages from various historical figures, the hacker is now sending short messages by text, in the form of a rap song and in a pop-up window.
Why do you think this change has happened?
Does it give us any better idea of what is going on?

What do you think is happening to Faye? Is she really changing, and if so, why?

The lunch that is described here is typical Brazilian food. See if you can find out what _feijoada_ is. Also, if you are interested in food, it might be interesting to look up manioc flour – it's used a lot in Brazil for making delicious sweet and savoury pastries. . .

In this chapter, Faye suggests that the purpose of the law is to defend citizens and make sure that everyone in society is respected. Can you think of an example that shows this to be true?

12 - Gregorio Alvarenga's Dedication

So it turns out that all the messages were sent by the same person, pretending to be different people, from Nefertiti to a whole lot of different Brazilian poets, and this person was at one time a wizard's assistant in the Middle Ages.

Would you say that that means it's all been a kind of ghost story?

The technician thinks the person calling himself Gregorio is nuts. So does Robbie but he is very polite to him. What do you think? Is he mad, or is he just unusually concerned about a rather strange idea?

Now that the Brainy Hacker has revealed what he wants, how do you think the kids will react? What would you do?

13 - Like a Movie

The students encouraged their teachers to read at the end of the story. Why is it important to have a library in the school, either for students or for teachers?

Gregorio, the Brainy Hacker, says that the written language allows human beings to travel through time and conquer death. What do you think he means by this? Do you agree with him?

Gregorio also talks about abandoning literature in favour of the image. What image is he talking about? Can you imagine what the world would be like if there were no books?

In this chapter, the author talks to you, the reader directly, and invites you to carry on the story. Why don't you give it a try? What might the characters do next?

Answers to Think About It
3 - The Brainy Joker Strikes Again

Andrea has a colleague called Colin.

Andrea is electric in the mornings, once she gets going.

Andrea is an intern in a law firm.

Carol is cross with her older sister for using her computer.

Carol understands Sonia's morning grumpiness.

Carol is the youngest in the family.

Colin is a lawyer.

Colin drives a car.

Answers to Quiz

1: Brasilia
2: Rio de Janeiro
3: Portuguese (or Brazilian Portuguese)
4: Yes, five times.
5: Samba
6: Coffee is Brazil's most famous export, but chocolate is also a good answer. (Brazil nuts also come from Brazil, of course, though they are probably not found in *every* home.)